FALLING FOR HIS FAKE WIFE

ALIE GARNETT

For my husband.

THE LOVELY'S

Sera Lovely Dean –36-year-old who is the Director of HR, Stepmom of 5 and mom of 2 finally married to Harrison Dean

Harper Lovely Hawthorn - 30-year-old who is a Sole owner of Lovely Catering and wife of Kaine Hawthorne.

Mabel Lovely Scott - 29-year-old who is a twin to Lucy, Children's Lit professor, married to Clifton Scott V. (whom she did not steal from her twin, despite what others have said.)

Lucy Maude Montgomery Lovely - 29-year-old twin to Mabel, is a Personal assistant, homebody who has cleaned up her wild ways. About to get the life change of a lifetime.

Agatha Lovely - 26-year-old who is an amazing artist and mediocre bartender looking for a job,

Buzz Lovely Raiden – 26-year-old who is married to Jones Raiden and who has finally found something she is good at, rich man's wife.

Frankie Lovely - 21-year-old College student in Chicago.

Louisa Raiden - 19-year-old College student in Chicago.

Emmaline Lovely – 16-year-old sullen teen with a newly minted driver's license. Who has been to one to many weddings and would like them to stop.

Violet Lovely – 8-year-old upbeat, outgoing artist who is loving every single wedding she gets to attend.

CHAPTER ONE

SLEET WAS HITTING the window in silent smudges of half rain, half snow. They were large drops, and Lucy Lovely wished she could hear the satisfying splats on the window. But the windows were sound-proof, so all she could do was watch. Even now, hours before the end of her workday, she was a little nervous about the drive home. Nobody seemed to be able to drive in this weather, no matter how many times a year it snowed.

Her phone suddenly shook in her hand, indicating she had a phone call. The sound almost made her jump. She was in her boss's office, looking out the window because her office didn't have one. Not that she wasn't allowed in his office, just that it seemed weird that she was in there when he was gone.

"Lucy," she answered curtly without looking to see who it was. But it was her personal phone, so it was someone she knew. If she had been answering her work line, she would have been friendly and personable. Today she was happy her boss was out of the office so that she could answer the call. She hated when she had to ignore it. Her friends and family seemed to avoid leaving a voice message, opting instead to send a text. She hated those even more.

"Hey, Lucy, it's Harper." Her older sister sounded breathless on the phone. The woman was always doing a dozen things during the day. "I need a big favor."

Lucy tried not to get her hopes up at the request. Eight months ago, she and Harper had been running a thriving catering business Lucy had loved. But once Harper had married Kane Hawthorn, head of Hawthorn International, she had been able to hire the people she needed to help her. Her younger sister was no longer needed or wanted, it seemed.

"Sure, Harper, what can I help you with?" Lucy kept the excitement from her voice. Maybe today was finally the day Harper would really need her back.

"When you get home, could you take out fifty pounds of chicken from the freezer and put it in the fridge? I'll swing by and grab it tomorrow morning. I've been keeping it there because I'm out of room here. It would help me greatly," Harper said. "Here" was her new house, the one she shared with her new husband. It was huge and gorgeous. "Home" was the big Victorian they used to live in together, where all her sisters used to live. Now they were mostly gone, married and happily living with their respective husbands.

Watching as the sleet blurred her view of the street below, Lucy tried to keep her voice steady. "Sure, I'll do it when I get home."

"Thanks, you're the best," Harper said and hung up on her in a rush. Lucy knew how rushed she used to be on days where they had an event. It seemed nothing had changed.

"Bye," Lucy said out loud to the dead line, not hiding the disappointment in her voice anymore. If she had been so great, she would have been helping her sister, not working here right now.

It had been six months, and she still missed her old life of being a caterer. The sisters had been partners for three years, or Lucy had thought that they had been partners. After a month where Harper was working another job, and Lucy had to take over most of the catering business, Harper had returned with a rich boyfriend and more time and money.

Still, Lucy had thought that they were partners in Lovely Catering. Then during a Saturday morning breakfast with all the sisters, Harper had let Lucy know what she thought of her and who she was in the company.

That morning, their mom, Sera, had been sitting at the island at the house the girls had been raised in, waiting for leftovers from the night before's catering event to warm up when she said, "There's a secretary job opening in the building next to me. The HR guy is looking for someone."

"Who wants to be a secretary?" Lucy's sister Agatha asked as she ate a freshly made cinnamon roll. Agatha was a bartender when she wanted to be, as well as a full-time artist. Sera was always trying to get her to be more than a bartender but always failed.

"I was thinking you." Sera herself was waiting on the pork chops that were still warming in the oven.

"Nope," Agatha responded quickly, as everyone knew she would. Agatha did not work during daytime hours.

Sera gave her a disappointed look and then looked at her other adult daughters. Agatha was out. Mabel taught at the university and was married, so she was out. Harper had just moved in with her billionaire boyfriend, so she didn't need a second job. Now she could be a full-time caterer. Buzz was still hanging on to her reporting career by her fingernails and wasn't even there that morning. That left Lucy, the lone one who could possibly take the job. So, all eyes turned to her.

Saying over the bite of cinnamon roll, "Me? No, I can't be a secretary."

"Of course you can, Lucy," Sera stated. She never saw any flaws in her children, even if Lucy's most obvious flaw for this job was that she could barely read. Having only known she was dyslexic for a few months, she had always just assumed she was too dumb to learn to read, not that she had a disability.

"I really don't think so," Lucy argued.

"I can put in a good word. If it doesn't work, it doesn't work," she said with a smile. Sera was the happiest person Lucy knew.

"I have a job. I work with Harper." Lucy pointed to the woman busy in the kitchen.

"I can do it without you, Lucy. I don't need you as much now that I can devote all my time to the business. I love having you help, but it would be a better job than cleaning," Harper insisted. Up until the week or so before, she had a full-time job and worked with the catering business, but so had Lucy—only hers was a cleaning job at an office near the house. Both had agreed that until the company took off, they would each have a second job. That was until Harper fell for Kaine.

Lucy looked over at her sister, her best friend and co-owner of the business she thought that they both ran. "What?"

"I was thinking that since I asked Kane to cut back, I should too so that we can spend more time together. It's only seems fair." Harper shrugged as if they had talked about it.

"I thought we were going to start doing more than one event at a time? Expand?" That had been all Harper could talk about for months.

"I know, but that was before. Now I think we should just concentrate on a few events a week, and I can handle that on my own easily." Harper took a pan from the oven, the new commercial oven they had just installed to grow their business.

Looking around the room, it didn't seem like anyone cared that Harper was changing everything in one instant, that they hadn't discussed it, and Harper was kicking Lucy out.

"But we worked so hard! We got The J!" Lucy said in disbelief. They had only been working the event venue for just over a week. They were finally making a name for themselves in the catering world. Calls had doubled last week, doubled!

"I don't think we can keep doing The J, especially without another chef. I can't make all the food for two events at a time." Harper must not have noticed that her words affected her sister.

Another chef, AKA not a cook. Lucy wasn't formally trained like Harper was. Harper had spent four years in Paris learning to cook in fancy restaurants. Lucy had spent that same amount of time at diners in town, learning to cook almost anything, but nothing fancy.

"So, we're just letting it go?" Lucy had worked for months to get them to be the first choice if the house caterers couldn't do it. Hours of calling and charming the manager, dozens of free samples she made without Harper even knowing about it, just so that Harper could have her dream—a dream she no longer wanted.

"Kaine and I thought that it was going to be too much for me, even with your help," Harper said, her attention on something else.

Lucy dropped the rest of the cinnamon roll onto her plate. She couldn't eat. Her sister had just told her that she wasn't equal in the business and had just been helping out.

"Send me the information about that job, Mom," Lucy said in defeat there was no changed Harper's mind once it was made up. With a sigh she got up she left the room. What did she have to lose? Her current extra job wouldn't pay the bills, and apparently, she was no longer a caterer.

Her mom must have had some pull because here she was six months later. Though she hated being a secretary, she was good at it. Actually, better than good at it; she seemed to be great at it. When she had started, it was for a lower-level executive and had been poached by the owner within three months.

Now she had worked on the top floor for Leonard Montgomery. From 8 a.m. to 5 p.m., she was nothing but the professional that Mr. Montgomery wanted her to be. And she even dressed the part in skirts or slacks and blouses with sweaters on top. Well, it had been winter almost since she'd started.

Lucy stamped her high heel into the carpet. She should have told her sister no, but she lived with the hope that one day her sister would want her back. That day was not today.

With one last glance out the window, Lucy left the office and sat down at her own desk. Flipping through the calendar on her desk, she knew nobody else could read it. She wrote it how she saw it, which was completely wrong and in capital letters. Mr. Montgomery thought she had a unique shorthand, but she didn't. It was just her being awful at spelling. Most of the time, she just had everything memorized and used the calendar for backup.

Like today, she knew Mr. Montgomery was in court with his ex-wife. They had been divorced for as long as she had worked for him, but not too long before that. The woman was constantly looking for more money and just messing with the amount of time Mr. Montgomery got to see his kids. It was just a waste of time, and even Lucy was tired of it. And Lucy was just the man's personal assistant.

Her eyes were still on the computer when the man himself walked into the office. Leo Montgomery hurried in with a file tucked under his arm. His black suit looked as fresh and crisp as it had five hours before when he had walked in for the day. His dark brown hair was still perfectly combed without a hair out of place. Nothing about his actions gave her any indication of how court went.

"Mr. Montgomery, is there anything I can do for you?" She hopped up and followed him into his office. As she did, she pulled the Bluetooth headphones from her ears that she used to have the computer read her the files she had to review and tucked them into her pocket.

"No, nothing, Lucy. Is there any coffee?" he asked, sitting behind his desk.

"Sure, let me get you some." She turned and walked back to her office, where the coffee pot was sitting.

Quickly, she went back to him with his cup in hand. Careful not to spill the hot liquid, she carried it to his desk and set it down where he liked it.

Over the last five months, she had enjoyed working with him, though he wasn't all that easy on his employees. But Lucy had nothing to lose and just let his comments roll off her back, from not calling her by the correct name to changing his requests in the middle of a conversation.

Sure, changing things in the middle of telling her about them had been annoying, but calling her Macy had been weird. It was eerily close to her identical twin's nickname, which was Maby. But it was also an odd combination of the two names. The nickname didn't bother her at all. When she started, she wondered if he had known her sister and was oddly combining their names but had later found out he never tried to learn a person's name for a few months.

"Do I have anything planned this evening?" He didn't pick up the coffee. Lucy wasn't surprised—he almost never did.

"Yes, you have a date with Jessica Henderson at 7 p.m. at The Detail." She sat down, perched on the chair in front of his desk.

"Are you sure?" he quizzed. He didn't really trust that she had his schedule memorized.

"Yes, Mr. Montgomery. Tomorrow you have dinner with Kelsey Murphy, but tonight is with Jessica." She bounced her left leg as she spoke, nervous energy that needed an escape route.

Yes, her boss had two dates in two days with two different women. That had been the pattern since she had started working for him. Lucy knew more women in this town than she had ever wanted to. Or at least their names.

"Did Ellington bring up the financials?" he questioned as he waited for his computer to come alive.

"No, but he emailed them to you around noon. Did you want me to print them for you?" she asked. They were trying to use less paper and more electronics, or so he said. Lucy still saw him with paper files all the time, though.

"No, I'll look on the computer," he mumbled as if computers were suddenly a new invention to him.

"Bill Handler from a real estate office also called. He emailed you some listings you might like. Are you selling your house?" She had been curious about that one.

"I would like you to keep my private life private, Lucy," he replied coldly, glaring at her with his almost black eyes.

"You know I will, Mr. Montgomery." She stared back at him, trying not to let the comment get to her but also wondering what was up with him. It didn't matter if he moved or not. To her, his house was only an address, one that she had memorized.

"Good. Now, if you could print off those financials for me," he said, once again changing directions in the middle of a conversation, wasting paper.

"Will do, Mr. Montgomery." Lucy got up and walked out of the office, leaving him to do whatever he did. It had been three months, and she still wasn't one-hundred percent sure what he did. So far, it hadn't mattered.

CHAPTER TWO

THE OFF-WHITE PANTS suit made Lucy Lovely look every bit the ice queen that she was. Cold and in command. She didn't even write anything down; she just knew the answer to everything. No matter how hard Leo Montgomery had tried to knock her off balance in the last few months, he had always failed.

When he had first seen her working for Bruce Vance in HR, he had wanted her, but not as his personal assistant. He would start with her as his personal assistant and move on from there. But she had never given any indication that she would be interested in anything like that. Maybe because she was in charge of his dating calendar, which was busy.

There was no ring on her finger, but she was married, and Leo did not sleep with married women. There were some lines he didn't cross even if he had slept around while married he had never slept with a married woman. He wasn't going to start now that he was single again.

For three months, he had gotten to know a little about Lucy and liked her a lot. It had taken only a week or two to see that she was not his type at all. He had never been turned on by cold, professional women, women who didn't know how to relax. And Lucy definitely did not know how to relax—he had never seen her anything but ready to work. That's how she was able to run his office better than anyone else, and she even took care of his kids' calendars.

With four kids and two ex-wives, it was a lot to handle, but Lucy managed to know where they all were and where they were all going. Aubrey was in her first year of college, and Alexis was sixteen and getting her driver's license. Addison and Amelia were in elementary school, dance, and karate. Lucy always knew who had what and when.

No matter how well she looked in heels and skirts, she wasn't his type, but he liked to look. Maybe too much. He liked that she never got comfortable in his office, perching on chairs or just standing. Sometimes she would pace, which bothered him, but he never said anything about it.

Today her long brown hair was hanging down her back in thick waves. It was rare that she wore it up. It was always long and gorgeous, not that he noticed.

Looking at his personal assistant saunter out of his office took his mind off the court date scheduled for that day. Stacy had wanted more money and to move the girls to Chicago. They were ten and eight now, and he didn't want them that far away from him. His older kids were here, and he wanted the four to be close one day. They needed to be living in the same town.

But after court, he was sure Stacy would take them away, which meant he would have to follow with the older two. He would have to move his entire life to keep them together, which was why Bill, his realtor, was looking into houses in Chicago.

At this point, he didn't need anyone knowing he was thinking of moving the company; the investors would not be happy if he did. But his family was more important than his company, no matter what either of his exes thought.

Lucy's voice came over the phone, "Kelvin is on line one."

Picking it up, he barked, "What happened, Kelvin?"

"I have told you time and again, she has the stable life. You're a swinging single and are acting it. A parade of women is not what your girls need to see, Leo."

"What can I do?" he asked.

"I have told you the simplest plan."

"I'm not getting married again. I'm not even seeing anyone that would qualify as a girlfriend, much less a wife."

"Stop screwing around and find someone for your kids. Maybe someone who doesn't care that you're screwing around? Someone who isn't emotionally invested in you as much as your girls," Kelvin offered.

Leo's mind went straight to the women he had spent time with recently, and no one fit into that category. They had been very interested in him, but he was sure none of them even knew he had kids. Or cared.

Movement in the outer office caught his attention as Lucy leaned forward in her chair. Even from this distance, he could tell that she had kicked off her shoes, leaving her feet bare and directly in his line of sight. Not that feet had ever done it for him, but he couldn't seem to take his eyes off hers.

For an instant, he regretted that she was most likely already married. Despite being an ice queen, she seemed to like his kids and asked about them every now and then. She even remembered their names and ages the few times they came to the office. None of his other secretaries had ever taken an interest in his kids, not even the ones he had slept with.

No, Lucy was happily married, and he had even seen her husband a time or two when she was running a little late, and he walked her to the car. She always had a laugh for him, a joke. It was the only times he had seen her show any emotion beyond a smile. But Mr. Lovely was lucky enough to get her laughs.

When she had moved up to work in his office, he had realized he should have checked Lucy Maud Montgomery Lovely's file a little closer. Two last names and a man meant "married" in every sense of the word.

Then once he had caught her on the phone, laughing with a Cliff. So, she was Mrs. Cliff Lovely, and Leo had made sure he didn't forget that. Ever.

CHAPTER THREE

"Are you ready to go, Lucy?" Harrison asked from the doorway.

Looking at the clock, Lucy realized that she had been working too intently on the report Mr. Montgomery had recently sent her. Pulling out the headphones, she put them on the charger she kept on her desk to be ready for the next day. It had taken less than a day to realize how much reading a secretary had to do, so she started using the headphones and having the computer read to her. It was a way to read without actually reading anything.

Ready to go, she was happy to see her stepmom's husband, even if her stepmom would have been a better sight, but Sera was two months pregnant, and it was an awful pregnancy this time. The first two had been a breeze for her.

"Yes." She sighed and closed down her computer. "How is it outside?"

"It started to snow, but it's melting as it hits the ground, so not bad yet." Harrison grabbed her coat from the tree and handed it to her. After knowing the man for seven months now, she liked him and loved him for her stepmom.

Grabbing her jacket from him, she slid it on and wondered what he thought when he looked at her, or any of her sisters, for that matter. The woman he was married to called them all her daughters but was only a decade older than the youngest of them. They should be peers, but each thought of the slightly older woman as their mom, always had. Her getting married hadn't changed that.

Leaving the office, they went a short distance to the SUV her mom was waiting in. It was warm by the time they got there, and Lucy was glad for it after the cold, windy walk.

"How was your day today, Lucy Maud?" her mom asked with a smile. Her mom was the queen of smiles.

"It went okay, Seraphina." She buckled her seatbelt and grinned. Her mom hated her actual name as much as Lucy hated being called Lucy Maud.

"Good. Mr. Montgomery wasn't too mean today?" she asked as Harrison pulled away from the curb.

During the first weeks of her job, Lucy had made the mistake to say that he had been mean to her. Her mom hated when people were mean to her kids; she was a mama bear. So, from then on, she always asked in case she had to set him straight.

"No, he was *great* today." She exaggerated on purpose.

"I think it snowed today because you both wore white." Harrison pointed at the two of them.

"Don't blame the weather on me, Harrison," Sera stated coldly. Her pregnancy had made her moody. Lucy wanted to laugh at her mom's husband; this was his first pregnancy with her. She was very emotional when pregnant, and he was just finding that out. Lucy had seen her through two already.

"Lucy, I think you have to take your mom out for drinks," Harrison usually didn't call the woman her mom.

"She can't drink."

"Maybe just get the girls together for some fun," Harrison restated.

"I will call." Sera sat up and pulled out her phone, already dialing, not noticing that the gathering was supposed to be for her.

"I just want my wife back in the clothes I sent her out in," Harrison told Lucy with a grin. They liked to change shirts when they got a few drinks in them, or none at all. Someone always had a better shirt on than someone else.

"I can make no promises, Harrison." Lucy's mom was her own person, and nobody could control her. He had been in her life long enough to know that.

By the time they dropped off Lucy at home, two blocks from their own house, the five sisters and one mother were going out on the town in an hour. Or at least to The Grog, which was the closest bar to Lucy's home—the house they had all been raised in.

The house was eerily silent as Lucy let herself in the unlocked door. It was never locked; even with only the two of them left living there, someone was almost always home. She worked days, and Agatha usually only worked at night. For years when there were eight people living there, the doors were never locked since people were in and out all the time. Sometimes the noise had been deafening, but not anymore.

After moving the requested chicken from freezer to fridge, she headed up to her room. No way was she wearing business attire to the bar. In the hallway, she hollered up the stairs to Agatha's third-floor layer, "Are you ready yet?"

"No, just a minute!" her little sister called. If Lucy didn't say anything, Agatha wouldn't be ready. In fact, if Lucy didn't drag her out the door in an hour, Agatha would blow it off.

"I have to change too!" she yelled and headed into the master bedroom, her bedroom now. Oddly, the entire floor was hers since Agatha hadn't moved down to the second floor when the other sisters had slowly moved out over the last six months.

She slipped out of the off-white skirt and hung it in the closet. A year ago, she would have just thrown it on the floor, but dry cleaning cost too much money to do that with her work clothes.

Grabbing a pair of low-rise jeans, she shimmied them on and was ecstatic that they still snapped. Running her hands over her slightly rounded stomach, she wondered when she would get the nerve to tell her mom she was pregnant, tell anyone for that matter.

It's not like she planned to get knocked up, but Harper's

announcement that she was no longer wanted at the catering business had sent her into a tailspin. Add to that her twin, Mabel, had married Lucy's best friend Cliff, which she was happy about, well almost completely. Except, the night that they had gotten married, she had ended up with her on-again-off-again boyfriend, Kevin. Just one night, she had said, "screw this and screwed him." That was five months ago now.

Pulling a gray T-shirt over her head, she hid it from everyone. Maybe they thought that she was gaining weight and didn't want to say anything. Their sister Agatha had gone from dangerously skinny to a normal weight in the last year, so it could be that they didn't want to say they noticed.

Monday morning, she had her first doctor's appointment. Somehow, she had to get out of the carpool with Sera that day. Maybe adding a haircut would be enough to throw them off. Not that she shouldn't just tell them the truth, but for some reason, she was scared to death to tell them.

Since her mom and her sister, Buzz, were both pregnant now, it wouldn't be the worst thing that she was too. But they would be disappointed it was with Kevin, who had no idea and never would. She didn't need him hanging around for the rest of her life. And he already had a few kids he didn't care about, so he didn't need hers.

Lucy topped her T-shirt with a navy sweatshirt that said "O hi" in yellow, which was not a spelling mistake but an error with the printing process. It should have said "Ohio" and was the most coveted shirt in the entire collection. Before she had realized she had dyslexia, she'd had a screen-printing business and had spelled everything wrong, making so many spelling mistakes that the family was constantly wearing clothes with misspelled words. Sometimes it still bothered her because they were *her* mistakes. Her T-shirt said "Can-can" on it.

Smoothing down the shirt, she knew her sisters would never ask for the "O hi" shirt. She loved it and had never given it up before. And a perk was that it hid her growing belly perfectly. Pulling her hair into a ponytail, she didn't even bother with a mirror; she didn't want to impress anyone tonight. She just wanted to spend time with her sisters and mom, like the old days.

Men had entered all their lives but hers and Agatha's, making getting together more difficult. After working with Harper for years, she missed her older sister. And the others always helped out being waiters when they could. Only Agatha continued since she was perpetually jobless. Lucy couldn't bring herself to help; it still hurt to be in the middle of it but not a part of it.

Out of her room, she headed up to Agatha's layer, carrying her navy tennis shoes that matched her top. Sitting down on the top step, she asked her sister again, "Are you ready?"

"Yes, Lucy," she said from her easel, not far from where Lucy was lacing up her shoes.

Looking up, she saw her dark-haired sister was indeed dressed the same as she was, except for her sweatshirt. Agatha was in a gray "Pen" T-shirt. Lucy wondered if it should have been "Penn" but gave up on knowing what she had meant at the time.

"Just checking. Sometimes you get distracted." Lucy waved at her easel. Agatha was the artsiest of the sisters, but they all had a bit more of the artsy side than the practical side.

"Do you really want to go?" Agatha asked, not moving.

Lucy turned and leaned against the railing, both shoes tied, hugging her knees. "No, I want to stay home and watch Dawson's Creek."

"Me too, minus the shitty TV show. Mom wants us to go out." Agatha still didn't move.

"I know. I'm not up for drinking, and Mom and Buzz won't be drinking," Lucy complained. Buzz was the baby of the family. Her real name was Beatrix and went by Bea to everyone, but the family got to call her Buzz.

Agatha changed the subject. "You should talk to Harper."

"What about?" Lucy tapped her fingers on her knees.

"Her latest chef quit," Agatha stated.

"She'll hire another one; she wants a chef." Lucy got to her feet. She didn't want to think about her past.

"She needs a cook, a good one." Agatha followed her as she headed down the stairs.

"No, Agatha. She doesn't want me; she never did." Lucy headed down another flight of stairs with Agatha on her heels.

"Are we walking or driving?" Agatha said as they made it to the main floor.

"Driving." Lucy had been on her feet long enough today. Heels suck!

Heading out the door, they drove Lucy's Jeep to the bar three blocks over. They should have just walked since they had to walk one block once they parked, but they just laughed at themselves as they walked into the bar. They all hated The Grog, but it was close, and the drinks were usually good. Also, they bought the expensive frozen pizzas, which Agatha and Lucy ordered four of. They were hungry and knew the others would be as well when they got there.

By the time the first pizzas showed up, Sera and Buzz had arrived. Buzz was going on and on about Jonas, her husband. Nobody was really paying attention to the redhead. Harper soon showed up alone and started talking about how overworked she was since her latest chef quit.

Lucy held her tongue and looked around the bar. It was very quiet for a Thursday, but it was still early. Trying not to groan, she saw her ex, Kevin, come in with a young chick. *More power to him*, she thought and ignored them as best she could.

As she tried, her sister Mabel sat down next to her. "That ass Kevin is here."

"I know, trying to ignore," Lucy said to her twin. Even at twenty-nine, they were identical. They both preferred the same hairstyles and mostly the same clothes. Tonight, Mabel's hair was also in a ponytail, identical.

"What an ass," Mabel said and handed Lucy a rum and coke, her usual.

"Just leave it, Maby. How's Cliff? Or is he here?" She looked around and ignored the alcohol on the table.

"No, he had a meeting tonight, so I'm having a girl's night," Mabel said about her husband. Before they had gotten together, he had been one of Lucy's best friends. Now she rarely saw him.

"Cliff and meetings? My, how you've changed him." Lucy grinned at her, loving that he loved her sister enough to change from the wild party animal she had hung out with for a year.

"I think he needed a little changing; he was crazy. As were you, and see where you are now? How's the office?" Mabel couldn't believe that she managed to keep her job as a secretary.

"Good, how is teaching?" Lucy turned it back to Mabel.

Mabel shrugged. "Good, I'm not working this summer."

"What? The dedication is gone?" Lucy teased. Cliff was a billionaire, so his new wife didn't really need to work if she didn't want to.

"Just going to work on my doctorate with no distraction," Mabel admitted and took another drink.

The pizzas were gone, and the sisters started to dissipate slowly. Mom and Buzz were the first to leave. They were pregnant and couldn't drink, so they didn't have as much fun as the others. Soon Harper also left without a word to Lucy. She had sat across the table and talked mostly to Buzz and Mom.

That left the twins and Agatha sitting at the table. Both Mabel and Lucy had limited themselves to one, both saying because they had to work in the morning. But Mabel didn't have more than one in a sitting since she admitted to have to drinking problem. Lucy hadn't even drank her first one, which was actually sitting on the floor at her feet; nobody noticed it had vanished.

"Your ass's girlfriend is drunk," Agatha pointed out from her side of the table.

Lucy turned and took notice of the young woman that was hanging on to Kevin. She was younger than twenty-one, that was obvious. But how was she so drunk then? And Agatha had been right—the girl was beyond drunk.

Looking closer at the dark-haired woman, it clicked: Mr. Montgomery's daughter! The oldest one, Aubrey, but she was only nineteen. Lucy saw her picture every day on his desk.

Turning to her sisters, she said, "She is my boss's kid. She's only nineteen."

"What?!" Mabel turned to look at her again.

"How do you know?" Agatha raised a skeptical eyebrow at her.

"Pictures. She stopped by a few months ago as well, but I see her picture every day," Lucy stated.

"Are you sure?" Mabel looked at the girl again.

"Almost certain." Lucy didn't look again; there was no need.

"I think she needs to go home, and not with the ass," Agatha said flatly.

"What's her name?" Mabel asked.

Lucy looked again. "Aubrey Montgomery."

"I love that your boss's last name is your middle name. So cute." Mabel gave her a little side-hug before she got up.

Watching her sister walk up to the couple, Kevin was pissed the moment he saw her. Mostly he thought that she was Lucy; he never could tell them apart. Within a few minutes of talk, Kevin stormed out of the bar, leaving his young date behind, staring at Mabel.

Both Lucy and Agatha headed over to Mabel to see what happened. The girl had sat down in a nearby chair and was staring at Mabel and then Lucy and back again.

"You were right. Kevin was her ride, so she needs to get home."

"I'll take her," Lucy said, not that she wanted to, but the kid needed to get home and not find Kevin again.

"Are you sure?" Mabel asked and pulled the girl to her feet. "Do you think your boss will think you took her drinking?"

"No, we don't even know each other. Just help me get her to the Jeep, and if you take Agatha home, I'll take her," Lucy replied, grabbing the girl's other arm, happy that she wasn't putting up a fight.

"Glad we took your Jeep. Nobody pukes in mine but me." Agatha laughed and led the way out of the bar, pushing people out of the way.

By the time they got her situated in the front seat, Lucy was tired of her boss's drunk kid. She kept asking where Kevin was and why he had left her. Lucy kept telling her Kevin left everyone all the time.

With a wave, she headed out to the address she had punched into her phone. She had Mr. Montgomery's packages and dry cleaning sent there all the time. She had it memorized, though she had never actually been there. And this was not the way she wanted to see his home.

Twenty minutes later, she was dragging the crying, complaining girl up the sidewalk. Pushing the doorbell, she saw the kid's face turn completely green. Lucy winced. She knew that look very well.

"How far is the closest bathroom?" she asked the teen, who didn't answer her.

When the door opened, she yelled to the person behind it, "Bathroom, now!"

Not that she missed Mr. Montgomery in tight jeans that made him look human and a plain green V-neck T-shirt that showed off an impressive tattoo on his arm. His hair wasn't even styled the same as during the day. He was yummy in the evening.

Without hesitation, Mr. Montgomery opened the door wide and pointed to a door ten feet from them. Lucy hoped the kid had ten feet in her. Grabbing her hand, she pulled Aubrey across the entryway and into the bathroom.

Just in time, the kid let go of everything she had drunk that night … and maybe a little more. It was a lot. With a sigh, Lucy grabbed her hair and held it as the kid puked.

CHAPTER FOUR

"LUCY?" Leo looked from her to his kid and back again.

"I was out with my sisters and found her like this. Her boyfriend ditched her, so I took her home," Lucy explained, still holding his kid's hair.

"Where at?" he demanded too harshly, but thankfully, she had been there when Aubrey needed someone.

"The Grog, just outside of downtown." She patted Aubrey on the back.

The doorbell had pulled him from his thoughts of how to move his entire life to a new city and how it would affect everything. His kids were with their respective mothers, and none were expected to come to his house until tomorrow night. The doorbell had been unexpected—as unexpected as his personal assistant in a sweatshirt that said "O hi" on it. Or in jeans that hugged her butt like they were made just to show it off. This was not the Lucy he had worked with for months now. Her hair was up in a ponytail, making her look like she was still in college herself.

"Never heard of it," he admitted, wishing his kid hadn't either.

"It's just a dive. We only go to it because we live nearby." She grabbed the hand towel and wet it.

"We?" He leaned against the door jam, wondering who she liked to go to bars with. Probably her husband.

She handed the wet towel to Aubrey and said, "My sisters. It was a girl's night. No men allowed."

"Cliff must have been disappointed," he said before stopping himself. He wasn't supposed to know her husband's name; she had never said it to him.

"No, he had a meeting tonight, I guess." She shrugged and took the towel back from the kid and tossed it in the sink. "I think she's done. For now, at least."

He looked at her, concerned. "How much did she have?"

"I don't know. I saw them come in, but at first, I didn't realize she was your daughter. It was only later that I saw it, her smile from the picture on your desk."

"You recognized her from a picture?" Her memory was amazing and surprised him every day.

"Sure, my sister made sure it was her. How awkward to bring home your kid and it not be yours." She laughed at the image. She had such a nice laugh.

"You were right; this one's mine. She's supposed to be at her mother's place," he replied. Kelly was going to hear from him in the morning.

"I'm not dragging her there. I have to work tomorrow," she said as if he wouldn't be there also.

"You can leave her here."

"She can't leave me!" Aubrey cried from the ground.

"I'm right here, honey." Lucy crouched down and rubbed the kid's back again. She was really good with either kids or drunk people. Her brown eyes looked up at him, and she asked, "Can I help her to her room?"

"Sure," he said, backing out of the room.

Lucy helped Aubrey to her feet and brought her out of the bathroom. Leading the way, Leo went up the stairs and to the girl's room. Lucy, for her part, just slowly pulled the girl all the way. In the bedroom, she made sure Aubrey was in bed and had her covers up to her chin.

His kid rolled in her bed away from her new friend, and Lucy got up and quietly left the room. He turned and followed Lucy down the hallway, not believing she had recognized Aubrey from her picture, but Lucy's mind was sharper than anyone he knew about detail.

At the landing, she asked, "Does she have school tomorrow?"

"Yes," he said. She would probably miss it after her evening, though.

"Then I suggest a cold bucket of water at 6 a.m. and send her off. Nothing says regret more than school after binging, and the Lovely wakeup is the best on those days." She grinned, and her eyes lit up.

"Lovely wakeup?" He liked when she talked about herself.

She just laughed and didn't answer him. "Cold water," she reminded him as she headed to the front door.

"How often do you get woken up that way?"

"Once a month, I guess. But you don't have to be drunk for it. Just sleeping." She let him open the door for her.

"The Lovely wakeup?" He marveled at the idea.

"Ironic since Lovely is our last name, and it is very unpleasant." She shrugged and headed out the door.

"Thank you for bringing her home."

"Just happy Mom wanted to go out drinking tonight, or I never would have been there." She headed towards the old Jeep in his driveway.

"Me too," he admitted, but she didn't acknowledge that she heard as she opened the Jeep's door and climbed in.

Within moments she was backing out of his driveway and driving away. Lucy, his secretary. His very *married* secretary. Married to Cliff in the meeting. But all his mind could think about was her wet and naked in bed.

CHAPTER FIVE

LUCY HAD CALLED out goodnight to Agatha, who was in her room drawing, on her way by as she went into her room and crashed. Lately, she had started to go to bed closer to nine than ten, but last night it was closer to midnight before she finally was able to sleep. Then all she could think about was Mr. Montgomery in his jeans and green T-shirt and the muscles and tattoos he wasn't hiding under it.

Today he was back in a suit, but she was still looking for the muscles she now knew were there. Really? Since when had she even been attracted to him? Never. Nor was she attracted to him now; she was just looking for some muscles. And maybe at his butt once in a while, which looked way better in jeans than slacks. She wouldn't have guessed he even owned a pair of jeans.

Walking into his office with his coffee, she put his butt out of her mind almost completely. "How is Aubrey this morning?"

Looking up at her, he blinked as if he didn't recognize her. Maybe he didn't. Her new low-rise dress pants were brown, and the top she chose to go with it was also a shade of brown, which she didn't notice until she was out of the house this morning. Not her best look.

"She didn't like the Lovely wake-up." He watched her put his coffee down.

"Nobody does. You just learn not to sleep in or get too drunk." She sat in her chair but didn't lean back.

"She rolled out of bed screaming, but it woke her up," he admitted with a chuckle.

"Agatha, my sister, comes up fighting. I've fallen down the stairs more than once getting away from her. If she isn't still drunk, you can't outrun her." She laughed as well. Agatha was quick and agile when she needed to be but slow as a sloth in regular life.

"I thought it was a Lovely thing?" he asked, an eyebrow raised.

"It is. Agatha is a Lovely also." This was getting weird.

"What do I have going on today?" he finally asked, getting away from the personal talk she usually hated. Nobody needs to know her business.

After telling him about his day, she was glad to get back to her desk and the file she had been looking at before Harrison had gotten there the day before. Not that it made much sense at all, but she would look it over and send it off. She was glad her boss was a perfectionist, and there were never any errors when they got to her desk.

By 5 p.m., she was ready to go and met the couple at the car. The ride home was quiet as Lucy let Sera and Harrison dominate the conversation. Watching the city go by as they went, she chalked up another week of her life as a secretary. She wondered how many more there would be. Closing her eyes, she was afraid it was a lifetime.

On Saturday morning, Lucy had slept in, letting Harper take care of breakfast on her own. She didn't want Lucy there anyway, so she hadn't helped in months. From her bed she could hear the others downstairs. No matter what happened and where everyone lived, Saturday morning meant breakfast at home.

Rolling out of bed, Lucy was glad the morning sickness was over. Those had been rough days. Now the baby was happy to just make her fatter every day. Pulling on black leggings and a red oversized T-shirt that said "File End" in green, she headed down the stairs to see her family.

In the kitchen, Harper was busy heating up chicken and had muffins on the counter. Lucy used to make the sweet part of the meal, but not anymore. Now Harper did it all. A few months ago Harper had made an off comment about how the rolls turned out, so Lucy stopped completely.

Lucy slid onto the end stool next to Buzz, who was eating a muffin. Her red hair was up in a curly knot on her head. "Hey, Buzzy."

"Good morning, Lucy. One of the few to wake up and only have a stairway to come down." Lucy gave her half her muffin.

"Mom isn't here yet?"

"Nope, Jonas went over to spend time with Harrison. She should be here soon," Buzz said. Her husband and Harrison were friends from college, and now the two men got together when the ladies did.

Lucy yawned and stretched. "Has anyone awoken Agatha?"

"Nope, don't want to be chased through the house." Buzz laughed, and Harper ignored.

"I'll go," Lucy said to get out of the room.

Glancing quickly at Harper as she left the kitchen, she wondered what she had done. It was Harper who didn't want Lucy to work with her anymore. It was Harper who had the loving husband and money to burn. Lucy was just doing what she needed to do to get by.

Up two flights of stairs, she debated just hiding in her room until someone else came or everyone left, whichever came first. But instead, she headed up to Agatha's room and knocked on the banister.

"Saturday, Ag. Time to go have family time," Lucy said, but she wasn't into family time today either.

"Not ready," Agatha replied from under the covers.

Sitting down on the bed, she wondered if they were both depressed because everyone left or because of other things in their lives. Agatha had been a hermit for over a year now, and Lucy just didn't feel like being around people anymore.

"You can sleep as long as you want tomorrow."

"Are you going to?" Agatha flopped down the covers from her face.

Lucy grinned. "Fuck yes."

"Who's here?" Agatha asked.

"Buzz and Harper."

"And now you are up here. Did Harper say something?" Agatha

asked, eyes still closed.

"She doesn't talk to me anymore … at all. I don't know what I did." She tried to hold back the tears.

"You got a job," Agatha offered.

"She told me to. She said she didn't need me. Didn't want me." Lucy wiped the tears away from her cheeks.

"Don't cry, Lucy. I don't know what her problem is. You two were so close for years, now this." Agatha sat up and pulled Lucy into a hug.

"All those years, she didn't want me there but couldn't get anyone better. Now she has someone better and doesn't have to pretend around me anymore. I've stopped trying," Lucy admitted, just letting Agatha hug her. They both needed it that day.

"Now you got me crying. Thanks, Lucy." Agatha pushed her away.

"Sorry, can't do anything right anymore. Get dressed, or there will be a bucket of water coming up next."

Heading to the steps, Agatha's voice stopped her. "How was bringing home the boss's drunk kid?"

"Good, no puke in the car. She made it to the bathroom. I don't recommend having a conversation with your boss over his puking kid, though. Not as much fun as it sounds." Lucy folded her arms and then unfolded them. It emphasized her stomach size when she did it.

"Don't worry. I'm against bosses in general." Agatha swung her legs over the bed and said, "When are you going to tell everyone?"

"About Aubrey?" She looked at her sister, puzzled. They probably don't care about the drunken teen. Maybe Mabel would since she had helped get her to the car….

"About…" Lucy let her voice trail off. Agatha just nodded at her stomach.

"I don't know what you are talking about, Ag," Lucy stated. No way did Agatha know. She headed down the stairs.

"You can't hide it for long, Lucy Maud. It's growing," Agatha called after her, and she continued down the stairs and went into her room.

Lucy slammed the door behind her and then leaned against it. *Agatha knew.* Who else knew? She had been so careful, but Agatha lived with her, and though it was a big house, it was hard to be quiet when it was empty.

Lucy stayed in her room until she heard Agatha go downstairs, then she waited to hear someone else come in the house. Nobody did, so she stayed. Sitting on her bed, she looked at her phone for anything fun. There was nothing.

Heading downstairs a while later, she was happy everyone was there. Even Mabel had made it. Nobody said anything as she walked into the kitchen, this time sitting down at the table since the stools were full. Letting the conversation flow around her, she laughed at the jokes and zingers that were lobbed.

At the table, she sat with Emma, who was fifteen going on "I hate everything." Today she had her headphones in her ears, but Lucy was convinced they were not on, that she was listening to everything. She was just as nosy as the rest of them.

When Sera had married Lucy's dad, she was already pregnant with Emma, though she was not their father's kid. By the time baby Emma had been born, daddy Lovely was gone, and nobody had seen him since. But the girls had loved their new baby sister, and they also loved the one that came seven years later. Violet was the perfect baby of the family at eight. Both of Sera's babies were dark-haired with blue eyes in stark contrast to their mother, who was blond and pale. Harrison had been the father to both by a fluke, and they both resembled him.

By the time everyone was starting to leave, Lucy realized she really hadn't talked to anyone, just listened to everything. It didn't seem like anyone noticed, and they left without mentioning anything about it.

"I'm going back to bed," Agatha said as she headed out of the kitchen, not mentioning what she had said in her room.

"I'm going to binge-watch Dawson's Creek," Lucy called after her sister.

"I will be avoiding you like the plague," Agatha replied from the stairway.

Lucy didn't see Agatha for most of the rest of the day and only saw her once or twice the entire weekend. She spent it on the couch watching TV and sleeping. Nobody said one word to her.

CHAPTER SIX

LEO WAS FUMING when Lucy hadn't been there in the morning. She didn't even call in. *What was she doing?* Leo wondered. After contacting HR, he had finally gotten her cell phone number and called her close to 10 a.m. She politely answered and reminded him that she had an appointment that morning and was off half the day. She had never taken time off before.

While he was in her personal record, he reaffirmed that she was happily married to Cliff Lovely, which was not actually in her personal file at all. In fact, her emergency contacts had been Sera Dean, mother, and Mabel Scott, sister. No husband was listed, but you didn't have to list your husband for that.

Since Thursday night, he hadn't been able to get her out of his head. Not that her being in a sweatshirt and jeans was sexy at all, but the contrast from her work attire to her home attire had been striking. He didn't think she went home and stayed in the same skirts and blouses she wore at work, but he had also never pictured her in tight jeans and sweatshirt that said "O hi" in a bar for a night on the town. It was her smile and laugh he couldn't stop thinking about. It was something she never did at work.

At five minutes to twelve, she came in the door, carrying a cup of coffee and her notebook. Her outfit was black slacks and a red sweater over a white shirt. Nothing overtly sexy, but on her, it simply was. Her heels were red to match the sweater.

"Sorry, I forgot to remind you I had an appointment this morning," she said curtly.

"I couldn't read it in your calendar," he replied. He hated that no one could read it, but usually, it didn't matter.

"Sorry about that." She shrugged as if to say she was not sorry at all.

"What else is on the calendar today?"

"Meeting with marketing at three, and then you have Addison and Amelia's recital tonight," she reminded him without taking her eyes off him. It always amazed him when she did that.

"I also have a meeting with Kelly about Aubrey," he stated.

"What time?" she asked but didn't get ready to write it down. In fact, she hadn't opened the notebook yet.

"Six, before the recital. Which I did remember also," he pointed out, as if one event would impress her.

Not that he was going to tell her that he hadn't actually remembered, that the recital had slipped his mind when he had been talking to his first ex about their daughter. How Lucy managed to keep everything straight, he didn't know. He sure as hell couldn't.

"Just remember that she's nineteen and has to learn some things the hard way," Lucy said. She had never given him advice before.

She even sounded sincere about it, like she actually cared. Though every time any of his kids came into the office, she made a point to make them feel special. It was just how she was.

"I'll try to keep that in mind." He looked at her, but she was looking out the window behind him. Her mind wasn't there today.

"Thanks. I have a sister her age, and Aubrey reminds me of her. Just tell her to stay away from the guy she was hanging on that night. He's not what a nineteen-year-old needs in her life," she said, tapping her toes. Some days she was like a kid who hated to be there, and her feet just wanted her to leave.

"I'll mention it. You know him?" he asked, and her toes stopped.

Lucy bit her lip a moment and then said, "I dated him a while back. He cheated on me, and I have no doubt that he'll cheat on her."

Suddenly, he hated this guy even more. No longer was it about him leaving his daughter in a bar. How could he possibly cheat on Lucy? What kind of man could find someone better than this woman? What kind of man was Lucy interested in? Where was Cliff in all this?

He had no idea what to say. "Sorry about that, Lucy."

"I just don't want her to get mixed up with him. She deserves so much better than him," Lucy stated, and he wondered why she had wasted her time dating a man not good enough for his daughter.

Her words warmed his heart. In that moment, he decided he was going to use her to find a woman exactly like her for him to marry. If she was this warm and caring, she had to know others just like her. Meanwhile, he knew of none that came even close to fitting that description.

He went out on a limb. "Lucy, if I change my meeting with Kelly today, would you be available for a working supper?"

Looking surprised, she said, "I guess. I drove today, so I'm available."

"Good, I can order something in. I want to talk to you and get your thoughts on something," he replied critically. She was going to help him with his plan to stay in the city. She would be perfect.

His plan was a little out of the ordinary, but he needed some help. There were just things he couldn't do alone.

CHAPTER SEVEN

AT 5 P.M., Lucy sat at her desk as she had since three when he left for the marketing meeting. Today she didn't even pretend to work; her mind was working too hard as it was. She wondered what the meeting was about tonight. At least he was going to feed her.

All she wanted to do was go home and crawl into her bed and pull the covers over her head and never come out. Her doctor appointment had been brutal. Not only had they done a lot of tests on her, but they also had taken almost all the blood she had in her body. The doctor had been mad that she hadn't seen a doctor yet, the lady taking her blood had been mad that she had small veins, and the lady with the ultrasound machine had been mad that she wasn't excited enough.

For her part, she had been mad at them all because she was convinced it was their fault that there was not one but two babies in there. Fuck, she was single and having twins. She had no luck at all.

This morning when she had woken up, she had four months left on this pregnancy. Now she had three because they were going to come early. Twins always did. They were identical like she and Mabel but were bouncing baby boys, according to the ever-so-happy ultrasound lady. She wasn't ready for one baby, and now there were two.

When Sera's youngest, Violet, had been a baby, she had Agatha stay home with her. Now Lucy was wondering how much Agatha charged for nannying. And it would be double for Lucy. *Great.*

And in the middle of the excitement—or lack of excitement—Mr. Montgomery had called, wondering where she was. She was able to say "at an appointment" instead of the truth: in hell. Even on the phone, she could tell he was angry at her as well; everyone was.

The nurse had been amazed at how small she was but assured her that at any moment, she would pop. Yup, she'd used the word "pop." All Lucy had to do was wait. She as going to be huge.

On the drive back, she had started to analyze her life. She had always just thought that when she had kids, she would be staying home with them. Even if her mom hadn't, or her real mom, for that matter. Her real mom had been a college professor and not too interested in her five girls.

But she would have to work because she had no one to help but Agatha. One day, maybe Agatha would meet someone, and she too would be gone. At least Lucy would win the house then, by sheer fact that nobody loved her.

"Sorry I'm late." Mr. Montgomery rushed into the office carrying his laptop and a few files in his arms.

"I didn't realize," Lucy admitted. She had been wallowing in twins.

"Did you order anything?" he asked from in his office.

"No, you said you would." She realized that had meant she would do it. He never did those types of things.

"I can. What do you want?" he asked, putting the files away.

"I'll do it. Just give me a moment." She turned back to her desk and wondered what restaurant would be fastest.

Within a few moments, she had pasta dishes coming in less than thirty minutes. Hoping that they were on time, she waited for him to call her into the office again. He was looking at his computer.

Back into her wallowing, she decided she would have to clean out Violet's room, but Violet was completely attached to having a room at home. Since moving two blocks down with her mom and dad, Violet and her sister, Emma, had both insisted on keeping a room at the house they had been raised in. Until now, it hadn't been an issue since there was plenty of room, but with Lucy having two babies, those rooms would be needed.

"Lucy, are you okay?" Mr. Montgomery was standing in the doorway, looking at her. She wondered how long he had been there, watching.

"Fine, thank you. Pasta will be here shortly." She covered her spaciness. Maybe a meeting today was a bad idea. By tomorrow, she might have a grip on the situation, but she was sure she wouldn't.

"Did you get my favorite?" he asked.

"Yes." She grinned because he liked that she rarely asked what he wanted. "Alfredo with chicken."

"Good, you know what I like. How do you remember everything?" he asked, not for the first time.

"I don't know, just can," she lied. Early on, she had learned that if she figured it out the first time, she wouldn't waste time looking again, so she committed it to memory. If she heard it, it was even easier.

"Did you get your hair cut?" he asked, looking closely at her.

"A little, just needed the ends cleaned up. Got it done right before I came back." She wondered why they were talking about her hair. It was after 5 p.m., and she wanted to go home. Her bed was calling her, the one with the nice covers to pull over her head.

"I think we'll go to the conference room. Did you want something to drink?" he asked, shoving his hands in his pockets as if he were nervous.

"Sure, a water or a pop would be great." She watched him walk out of the office, most likely to the break room where the machines were.

Soon he was back, but empty-handed, and his hands were still stuffed in his pockets. Back in his office, he hurried with a file and said he would wait in the meeting room. This left Lucy alone to wait on their meals. He was acting strange this evening; well, actually, he'd acted strangely most of the day. Or maybe he'd been acting weird since she had taken Aubrey home that night. He was probably going to talk to her about being around his daughter.

She had just started pacing when their meals came, probably

because she was not ready to have a meeting about how she was a bad influence on a teenager. Taking the two white containers down to the conference room, she found him pacing also.

Once she was in the room, he sat down, and she handed out the meals. Opening her container, she was happy she chose the stuffed shells. She loved to make them and eat them, though she hadn't made them in almost a year now. A few weeks before, the leftovers on Saturday had been stuffed shells, but Lucy hadn't been able to eat them, and it wasn't the babies that were holding her back.

"Lucy, I need to know that everything we say tonight will be confidential. I do not need anything we talk about to get out," he started. His fork was still lying on the table beside his food.

Stopping mid-chew, she nodded in agreement. She was hungry, okay?

"I would have you sign something, but I think I can trust you," he continued, and she stopped eating. Signing papers was a serious thing.

"What's going on, Mr. Montgomery?" she asked, finally setting her fork down. She hoped he wasn't firing her. She was having twins now, and this job was all she had.

"Leo. You can call me Leo when we're alone," he said, and her eyes went up to his. Did he even look like a Leo? This was going to be hard.

She tried the name out. "Okay, Leo." Maybe that wasn't going to be as hard as she'd thought. The name made him more human, and it was better than Leonard.

"I don't know if you know that Stacy wants to take the two little girls to Chicago," he stated.

"No, I didn't know. I know you go to court a lot, but just that." Actually, she didn't care what happened in his personal life. She was his secretary, so her only concern was what happened here at the office.

"If the judge agrees, I'm going to move the company to Chicago. Aubrey is basically an adult, and Alexis is sixteen, but the little two are young, and I don't want to lose contact with them," he explained.

"I understand about the children, but won't it cost a lot of money to move the company?" She leaned back in her chair.

"It will, but they're my children, my first priority."

"As they should be. The girls should be together, but I regret that you would leave the bigger girls when you go. I was raised in a house full of girls, and I'm having a hard time with them moving out, and we're adults." Her mind went to the day each had packed their belongings and moved in with their new man. Mabel had been the hardest. She was first, and she was her twin. The empty room across from hers had been hard to look at for months.

"How many girls?" he asked with his head slightly tilted.

"Seven in all." She grinned; it was a lot of women. And it didn't even count the two sisters that they had just found out about a few months before, girls that their birth mom had after leaving the older five behind. It was still new, and they both lived in Chicago, so they weren't part of the count in Lucy's head yet.

"Well, I don't have that many, but I would like them to be close. But I have to follow the ones that need me the most."

"What can be done to stop Stacy from moving?" she asked.

"My lawyer said that my life is a revolving door of woman and that a judge would be more favorable to give Stacy custody rather than me," he admitted.

"It is. I make those reservations. But what can you do to change that?"

"A wife," he said, then pushed his container of food away. "And I want you to help me find one."

"What?" She didn't see that coming at all.

"You know women, and I need a woman who can take care of my kids, be responsible for my household, and stay married to me no matter what. The judge needs to see I'm in a happy, healthy relationship." His eyes pleaded with hers.

"What are you looking for?" she asked. She didn't know that many people, and the ones she did were not who he was looking for. Mom would have been perfect for this; in fact, she had almost done it before when she had married Lucy's dad. Though as far as Lucy knew, that was supposed to be a real marriage. But now she had Harrison.

"I don't know. I have a type, but I don't want that kind of woman. I want someone who can make a meal, make a birthday cake, drive the kids around, and look the part," he explained.

"For how long?" She rubbed the back of her neck. This was going to be impossible.

"I was thinking a year, but what about until Amelia graduated? I don't know...." He sounded like he hadn't put a lot of thought into it.

"So, one to eight years." Her toes were tapping; she wanted out. "What about sex?"

"What about it?" he asked in defiance.

"Well, do you want to have sex or not? With her, I mean." She knew her face was red; she could feel the heat. But then again, she was talking about sex with her boss, her sexy boss with the hidden tattoos.

"Up to her. I can get it elsewhere if I need to. I can be discreet about it." He leaned back in his chair and grinned.

"I hope you're more discreet about it than when you were married to Stacy," she said, tapping her fork on the table. His affairs had played a big role in the divorce, something even Lucy knew.

"Me too." He didn't seem to take offense at the accusation.

"What about if she has kids? Is that okay?" The tapping continued.

"How many?" he asked.

"I don't know! I'm just getting the parameters down."

"One or two kids, maybe. Prefer no kids, though," he said, looking thoughtful.

"What about if she wants kids?"

He shook his head. "No. I'm not having more kids."

"How old?" she asked.

"I said no more kids," he stated a little too loudly.

"I mean, how old do you want *her* to be?" Lucy tried to hide her grin. He was getting defensive.

"Thirty to forty-five, maybe? Try someone on the younger side. Maybe thirty to thirty-nine instead."

"Okay, how long do I have?" she asked, letting the fork fall to the table.

"Let's see if you've found someone by Friday."

She raised an eyebrow. "What happens if I don't?"

"Let's say this. If you have a name by Friday, there will be a twenty-five-thousand-dollar bonus. If I marry that person, you will get a total of one-hundred grand," he said coolly. Apparently, money meant nothing to him.

But for her, one-hundred grand bought a lot of two of everything. "Okay, let me see what I can come up with. Can I ask you more questions after this meeting, or is this a meeting room discussion only?"

"You can ask me questions, but shut the door. We'll meet again like this on Friday."

"Pasta again?" She pointed at the uneaten containers.

"Yes." He agreed, as if the next meeting they would be relaxed enough to eat anything either. Her stomach was rolling, but not with hunger.

Getting up, she left the room and headed for home. She had a lot of things to think about; a lot of people to think about. Nobody was coming to mind, though. Just her and Agatha, and no way was he Agatha's type. Agatha loved her a skinny, rocker guy, a little on the scuzzy side. But Agatha couldn't cook. That left her on her list of two, and she wasn't going to marry her boss for any amount of money. Not just because he had actually said he would probably sleep around on whomever it was. More because he wasn't her type either.

CHAPTER EIGHT

By Wednesday, Leo wished he had told Lucy he needed to be kept up to date about the wife search, that she needed to have a running list of possibilities that he could look at and analyze. Not knowing was driving him crazy.

Today she was in a navy skirt and white blouse and had a light blue sweater over the top. Though the skirt showed off her legs, the sweater reminded him of something his mother would wear.

At 11 a.m., she came in as usual, empty-handed, and said, "You are to be at Mario's in half an hour."

"Thank you, Lucy. I got distracted," Leo said, not mentioning he was distracted by her. Today her hair was up in a loose bun. It was a new look on her, a look he liked.

"That's why I'm reminding you," she said, tapping her black heels on the carpet.

"Is the car waiting?" he asked, knowing it was.

"Yes." She didn't expand. She didn't have time for him today, he could tell.

"I need you come with me." He got up from his desk, grabbing a folder that he was bringing to the lunch meeting.

"No, Mr. Montgomery. I don't do shorthand," she said. She never did shorthand. Not that he needed someone who could at the meeting, or anyone else for that matter. But he suddenly wanted her there.

"No shorthand, just remember what happened at the meeting and remind me when we get back. And there's a free meal."

"I can assure you that you don't want me there," she argued, even as she followed him from the office. Except it was her job to do what he wanted her to do, so she followed.

He handed Lucy her coat from the coat rack and pushed her out the door. In the elevator, she slid the jacket on her shoulders and sighed, not hiding that she wasn't happy to be there with him.

On the street level, the town car was waiting for him. Holding the door for her, he watched her slide angrily into the car. As he slid in beside her, he wanted to take her hand in his and reassure her that nothing was going to happen, but he didn't.

Her long legs were crossed, and the one in the air was tapping as they weaved through traffic. He wanted to grab her foot to see if it would stop her but assumed it would just piss her off.

"Who am I meeting?" he asked, opening the file.

Her eyes were looking out the window as the car drove, and she didn't answer the question. Just remained angrily silent.

"Lucy, do you know who I'm meeting with?"

"Yes, but so do you. I don't have to tell you," she barked out at him.

"Maybe you can just enjoy getting out during the day," he said.

She rolled her eyes. "I like staying put during the day. I have no reason to be at this meeting."

"I want you there, and that's the only reason I need to give," Leo hissed at her. Her anger was making him angry.

"Fine." She folded her arms, then unfolded them just as fast as she did it.

"I told Aubrey to stay away from that boy, but I don't think she listened," Leo stated a moment later.

"Boy?" She turned in her seat and looked at him. "Kevin is over thirty, Mr. Montgomery. Not a boy. He acts like it, but he is not a boy."

"What? She said he was twenty-three!" Leo stared at her.

It made sense that the guy was older than twenty-three. Lucy herself was nearly thirty and wouldn't date a guy that young. And she had been married for some time, so there was that.

"God no. He's thirty, possibly thirty-one. So, I wouldn't just let her date him. I would tell her that he is too old for her," Lucy replied as the car pulled to a stop in front of the restaurant.

"Don't worry, I will be talking to her about him again," Leo assured her, sliding out of the car and reaching out to help her out.

Tentatively, she took his hand. "Tell her to go back to campus and grab any guy there. They would be way better than Kevin."

Trying to ignore how warm and delicate her hand was, he had no response to his daughter dating a thirty-year-old. It turned out he didn't have a chance to say anything as the hostess took them directly to the table that Michael Hanover was sitting at, impatiently waiting for them.

Lucy ordered the special, not even bothering to look at the menu. Nor did she look at her phone, which he was happy about. Phones at business meetings were very much frowned upon by him. She just sat, not participating and not paying much attention.

As the meal and meeting came to a close without an agreement, he was disappointed that he had even gone to the meeting. Michael wasn't ready to make a deal, and Leo wasn't ready to push him yet. Soon, though.

Once Michael walked away from the table, he was left with a still-angry Lucy. Looking at her across the table, she was glancing around the room, more interested in what the waiters were carrying around than what Michael had been saying.

"What do you think?" he asked to make conversation.

"That they should stop serving so much salad. Nobody eats it all. It's just a waste of food." Her brown eyes turned to him as she said it.

"About the meeting?" he asked and leaned back in his chair. He tried not to grin.

"I have no opinion, Mr. Montgomery," she stated coolly.

"What if you *had* an opinion?"

"Based on this one meeting, I would still say I have no opinion."

"You have proofread half a dozen proposals I've sent him." Leo folded his arms.

"I don't really read those; I just proofread them. I never went to school for business, so I have no idea what I'm looking at," she admitted, though she knew more than she let on.

"Still mad I brought you then?" he stated the obvious. So much for her confiding in him about her search.

"Yes, I have no place here. Nor do you; he's not selling his company to you." She crossed her arms again, then quickly uncrossed them and reached for her water.

"Lucy?" A woman who approached their table asked. "Harper's sister, Lucy?"

He turned to look at the dark-haired woman in a smart business suit who was looking down at Lucy. Lucy turned to her with a smile, a smile she hadn't given him all day. "Yes, I am. I'm Lucy."

"I thought it was you, but I couldn't be sure you were Lucy. We missed the latest wedding in your family. Arabella joked that we just have to wait another month, and there will be another." Bex Carter chuckled, not acknowledging Leo at all. He knew she worked for Hawthorn International in marketing, and she most likely knew who he was.

"I think that one was the last for a long time." Lucy smiled even brighter. "How are the babies? They must be adorable."

"Yes, they are. Arabella is loving it. I think it's a lot of work. When I saw you, I had to say hello and see if it really was you," Bex said.

"It's me." Lucy didn't seem to notice that the question was weird.

"I was thinking it was you since Mabel works for the university. I just wanted to stop and say hi. I have to get back to work. Nice to see you again, Lucy," the woman said and walked away, not once saying a word to him.

"And who was that?" Leo asked.

"It doesn't matter. My personal life is personal," she said back to him. Meeting a friend while out of the office hadn't improved her attitude.

"You knowing the marketing director at Hawthorn International is not something you should be hiding," he replied. If she needed to name drop, that woman was a good one.

"I know more important people than Bex Carter, but it doesn't matter. I have no plans to use my connections to get ahead in the world."

"Only you would feel that way."

"No, Mr. Montgomery, I can assure you that there are others like me out there. Are we done here?" She pushed her half-eaten meal away from her.

"Yes, we are, but I think that you should first explain why you think he's not going to sell his company to me."

"Because he's just trying to get a higher price from somewhere else. Dropping *your* name gets that price up."

He tilted his head slightly. "Why do you say that?"

"He managed to get you to agree to a different number three times and still is not saying yes. He doesn't want to sell to you. Just give up and look elsewhere," she informed him.

"Maybe I should look at Hawthorn since you have an in there." He leaned back in his chair as he watched her.

"Kaine Hawthorn will never sell to you either. I wouldn't even try." She got up and headed for the door. The ice queen had earned her name today.

Getting up, he followed her. She had paid attention to what was going on and made up her mind about what was happening. She might be right about both companies, but he wasn't going to let go of the idea of owning either one of them.

CHAPTER NINE

SOON AFTER THEY returned to the office from their business lunch, Mr. Montgomery was out until 5 p.m. at another meeting. He'd probably be gone for the rest of the day, which was fine with her. She was tired of racking her brain for a suitable wife for her boss. But actually, days ago, she knew she didn't know anyone who would fit into his life.

The perfect woman who would be a dutiful wife and let her husband cheat just wasn't out there. Or at least not in her circle of friends, even though they were just a group of slutty girls and her sisters. Most of whom were now married.

So much for the money that she needed for the babies. So far, she hadn't gotten up the nerve to tell her family about them, but it would have to be soon. If Agatha knew, then maybe others suspected, which would make it less of a surprise.

Leaning back in her chair, she tried to decide who she should tell. Which one of her sisters was most likely to tell everyone else so that Lucy didn't have to? The obvious answer was her oldest sister, Harper. She couldn't keep secrets. But that was the only sister Lucy no longer talked to. Because as much as Harper was a blabber, she also wouldn't be afraid to tell Lucy how disappointed she was with her.

That was a conversation she didn't want to have, so she then decided maybe her best bet was to tell Maby. Maby and Cliff wouldn't lecture her; they would be nothing but excited about her having a baby —or even two. Except they would be disappointed because they would know exactly who the father was, so they might not be as excited as Lucy wanted them to be.

Dismissing her twin, she moved to Buzz, who she also dismissed out of hand. She was a newlywed who was adjusting to her new life. It hadn't even been a month since she had become Mrs. Jonas Raiden, and she was enjoying it. She talked about it way too much.

Which left her stepmom, Sera, who was being overly emotional now that she was pregnant herself, but she was probably who Lucy should tell first. She was the closest thing to a mom Lucy had, and this seemed like something to confess to a mom.

At just after 3 p.m., Leo's second ex-wife, Stacy, walked into the office trailed by two little kids. Mrs. Montgomery number two was a piece of work. She was always after a few more dollars. Oddly, if she had just stayed married to the man, she wouldn't have to spend so much time trying to get it from him.

"I have the girls here for Leo's night with them," she stated to Lucy. She pulled the power play every few weeks just to mess up his plans. Usually, he was there to fight his own battles.

"I don't believe he has this on his calendar," Lucy replied, looking at her calendar. She didn't need to, though. He rarely had them during the week.

"I don't think you really know, Lucy," Stacy said her name as if she was disappointed in her.

"Mr. Montgomery isn't even here. He's in a meeting," Lucy argued with the woman.

"I will just leave them with you, then. You work for him, so you can watch the children," she said, not looking at her two kids, who were clearly not excited to stay with a stranger.

With that, the woman walked out of the office, leaving behind the two girls who didn't want to be there with an adult who didn't want them there either.

Turning to two girls, she did what her mom would do in this situation. "Do you guys want to color?"

"No." The oldest, Addison, shook her blonde head at her. The other didn't answer at all. Though the two looked very similar, they didn't take much after their father with his dark, good looks. They were all their mother, sadly.

"Are you sure? I have an amazing collection of colored pens and even a box of crayons." She pulled them out of her desk.

"When will my dad get back?" Addison asked, not looking at the crayons.

"Around five," Lucy said, but if his meeting ran late, he wouldn't come back here at all—he had a date with Nadine tonight. Lucy hoped he would find the one in Nadine, and for some reason, still give Lucy the money he'd promised.

"Shall we see if there's something on the TV in your dad's office we can watch?" Her sixteen-year-old sister, Emma, would be into that activity, though eight-year-old Violet would be all into the colored pencils. She had never realized how easy her little sisters had been until this moment.

Both went for the TV, and she went into the empty office and hoped he had cable. After a few minutes of messing around with it, she knew he didn't, but she had it on her phone and had managed to hook her phone up to the TV. Suddenly, they had a lot of options.

By 5 p.m., she had raided the vending machine and called her mom that she had to work late. When Leo finally arrived, she would just take an Uber home.

By 6 p.m., she had given up on him showing up at the office and had left a message on his phone about the girls. After that, she ordered pizza for them and let them run around the building to let off some energy that the sugary snacks had brought.

An hour later, she called Agatha for a ride. Her sister wasn't busy, so she came and picked them up. Lucy left another message on Leo's phone.

By 9 p.m., Lucy was snuggled on the couch with a sleeping Amelia lying almost on top of her, and Addison was holding on to wakefulness by her fingernails. But then again, so was Lucy. Kiddy TV shows were the worst.

By 11 p.m., she had put the girls to bed, each in their own room because of the number of empty bedrooms in the house. They were sound asleep, and so was she when her boss finally called her back—her very angry boss.

"Lucy, it's Leo Montgomery," he barked as if she didn't know who he was. "Where are you? Do you still have my kids?"

"Oh, you're alive. I had given up on you and decided to raise them as my own. I don't even think they remember you," Lucy said sarcastically. She'd never used that tone with him, before but she was tired and couldn't be "office Lucy" right then.

"Where are you?" he asked a little more nicely, but not much.

"I took them home with me. They're sleeping now, so I'll bring them home in the morning."

"That's okay, I'll come and get them now," he said curtly.

"Mr. Montgomery, the girls are very tired, and they're already asleep. I will bring them home in the morning," she stated and hung up on him.

Tomorrow would be soon enough for the girls to be reunited with their father ... and for her to be fired. She should have just taken his kids home when he asked—a good assistant would do that. Except she wasn't a good assistant.

Trying to get back on her boss's good side, Lucy had the two girls out of the house and on the road home by 6 a.m. the next morning. Since she had been unable to sleep much that night worrying about her job, she had been up early and made cinnamon rolls, something she hadn't done in months.

It used to be her specialty before Harper took over family breakfasts. Now there weren't always cinnamon rolls or any sweets since Lucy hadn't felt welcome to make anything since she'd quit working for Harper.

So, with fresh cinnamon rolls, she took the girls to their father. So far, she had more than one of his kids in her Jeep over the last few weeks. It was starting to be a weird habit for sure.

Addison and Amelia were happily eating a second roll when she pulled into their driveway as the sun was starting to come up. She didn't know when Leo expected them home but didn't think it would be this early.

Amelia ran with her sticky fingers to ring the doorbell since the girls didn't have a key. By the time Lucy made it to the door, they were taking turns ringing it, neither letting the bell stop ringing before hitting it again.

The little girls were giggling and pushing the doorbell until the door finally opened to let them in. Leo Montgomery was in just sweatpants and nothing else: no shirt, no socks, no nothing. Lucy was finally able to see his entire tattoo, and it was very nice. As nice as the abs she hadn't suspected. Lucy realized he was hiding a lot under those suits.

"Cinnamon roll?" She held them out. Clearly, the guy had just rolled out of bed and looked like he wanted to get back in it.

"Not yet." He crouched down to hug the two girls who had missed him, but he was looking at Lucy as she shut the door behind her.

"They're good, Daddy. Lucy made them all by herself!" Addison told her father.

"They smell good," he commented as he scratched at the dark stubble on his chin and got to his feet.

"I had two," Amelia said.

Lucy smiled. "I'll just leave them with you for the other two girls and you." She held out the pan to him. Somehow, she had expected him to be in a suit at the crack of dawn.

"Thanks, but it's just me this morning." He took the pan from her, but his eyes were on her chest as he did it, making her wonder if she had gotten something on her gray sweater, but she was not checking in front of him.

"I got to sleep in Lucy's old room. She has a new one now," Amelia chatted excitedly, not that Lucy's old room was exciting at all.

"I got Harper's room. It's green, and I love green." Lucy smiled again. After hours together, they had finally warmed up to her.

"Why don't you two go change out of those clothes since you slept in them," Leo said, nodding at the stairs.

"We didn't! We slept in Lucy's T-shirts!" Amelia replied happily but headed into the house anyway.

"What time did Stacy drop them off?" he asked her.

"Three p.m., just when they got off from school. We stayed at the office until seven, then my sister picked us up and took us to the house," Lucy said, then added, "I started calling you right away."

"I saw that. I thought you were just texting about some work thing," he admitted as his eyes swept over her body again.

What was it about him today? Get him out of a suit, and he was all man, and oddly, checking her out? She was checking him out as well, but he was nearly naked. She was in work clothes.

She was lingering by the front door, not wanting to get comfortable around him when he was half-naked.

"I'll compensate you for last night. I hope it didn't wreck any of your plans," he said.

"I had nothing planned, but I had wanted to go home at a decent hour. I'll send you a bill," Lucy said, trying to be sarcastic. She didn't want to leave the gorgeous man in front of her.

"Do you want some coffee?" He was standing bare-chested, holding a pan of cinnamon rolls. She couldn't keep the images out of her head of ditching the coffee and rolls and following him back to bed.

"Uh, no. I'm not really a coffee drinker," she stated quickly, pushing the images out of her mind. He was her fucking boss! And he was a cheater—no way was she going there … again.

"I didn't know that. I guess I have never noticed. Sorry." His eyes came back to her face after another quick trip south.

"I'm just happy the girls are where they're supposed to be," she said and turned to leave.

"Why don't you take today off? Make up for the evening you didn't get," he said as she went out the door.

"I will do that." She silently cheered at her good fortune, a day to figure out someone for him to marry. Maybe then he would stop looking so sexy to her.

On the way home, she called Mabel to see if she wanted to spend some time with her today. They didn't get together as much as they used to. To her surprise, Mabel was free for the morning, and they would meet at the house.

Maybe Lucy would get the courage to tell her sister about the babies. It would be a perfect time for them to talk.

Lucy had barely got her clothes changed before Mabel was yelling up to her that she was home. Bounding down the stairs, she yelled up to Agatha to see if she wanted to join them. The little sister's answer was silence.

Downstairs, Mabel was already on the couch with a remote in her hand. Lucy sat down on the opposite side of the couch and waited for their favorite show to start.

"How are you and Cliff? I really didn't see you two getting along," Lucy said as the first episode started. It was something she asked a lot since the two fell in love six months before. She was used to it now, but it was still weird that her twin was married.

"It's going great! I found my other half. With him, I am whole. He makes me more outgoing, and I make him a little less wild. Like you used to do for me. You need to find someone like me." Mabel curled her legs under her and stared at the TV.

"I'll never find my Mabel," Lucy said with a sigh.

"You always just date people like you: loud, wild, listless guys. You need a stable one to ground you," Mabel replied.

"I think I'm off the market for a while." Lucy saw her opening but couldn't bring herself to tell her twin about her own twins. Today she didn't want to talk about all the ways she had messed up her life or all the things she had to figure out in such a short amount of time, from finding Leo Montgomery a wife to figuring out her life as a mother.

"That's when it happens, Lucy." Mabel grinned at her and snuggled into her just like old times. "When you least expect it."

"Not for me." Lucy had no intention of even looking for love for a long time now—a very long time.

The twins cuddled together on the couch, watching their favorite show. Agatha had come down at one point but just rolled her eyes at the twins crying and went back to her room. After Mabel left at 2 p.m., Lucy grabbed a notebook to write all the names of possible wives for Mr. Montgomery. By the last episode, Lucy was crying and yelling at the TV that Joey picked the wrong man, which always happened. If Mabel had still been there, she would have been cheering on the happy couple.

The forgotten notebook beside her was still completely empty. There wasn't even a line on the page yet. Lucy saw her twins' money slip through her fingers.

CHAPTER TEN

By Friday afternoon, Lucy had not asked any further questions, and she gave no indications she was even thinking about finding Leo a wife. He assumed she was and was keeping the information to herself per his request, but he had wanted her to talk to him about it some.

All week, her husband had picked her up again. On Tuesday, she had some comment the moment he arrived, and then on Thursday, neither said anything but just headed out together in calm silence. Sadly, that was what he wanted in a wife; someone to talk and laugh with and be silent when they wanted to. So far, he hadn't told her that that was also a part of the requirements.

Because if he'd added that, he would've also added that she needed to have a nice ass and long legs. Silky brown hair was a plus also, and brown eyes that knew his every move. But the married Mrs. Lovely was off the table. He wondered if she had told Mr. Lovely about her new job. He knew she did because they had no secrets. That's the kind of marriage Lucy had ... the kind of marriage he wanted.

As the clock struck 5 p.m., he headed out to her office. "Are you ready, Lucy?"

"Ready as I'll ever be, Mr. Montgomery," she answered, spinning in her chair towards him. Her gray slacks were more loose-fitting than her usual pants, and her blouse wasn't tucked in like she usually had it. Shrugging, he led the way to the conference room.

"Right in here." He opened the door for her.

She hurried past him, and he smelled her perfume and wondered what it was. It was light and flowery and made him think of her. He could tell when she'd recently been in his office; her smell lingered.

"I didn't order anything. I didn't think either of us could eat," she admitted what he had already realized as she cleaned off the table last week.

"That's okay." He pulled out her chair and went and sat in one at the end of the table.

"I only managed to come up with one name. I really tried, but I realized my friends are not the type of people you would want to marry. Screw around with, yes, but not marry." She shrugged.

"One might be all I need." He pointed out, trying to hide a grin. She looked defeated by the task.

"I have a few questions before I say who it is," she said, tapping her fingers on the table.

"Okay, go ahead."

"First, she's not yet thirty. Will that be an issue?"

"A few years under is no issue." He shrugged, maybe he was putting too much emphasis on age when in the end it wouldn't matter. It wasn't like they were going to grow old together.

"Next, she has no children but is currently pregnant, so she'll have them during the marriage."

"That might be an issue. If my name is listed on the birth certificate, then I'll be financially responsible for them. Wait? *Them?*" He turned to her, confused.

Lucy nodded quickly. "Twins. Couldn't there be something written up that says you are not responsible? Like a prenup for babies? Or what if your name isn't listed on the birth certificate?" she asked, her mind looking for a way around it. She was always thinking.

"No, but then again, I'll obviously get to know the kids, so maybe I'll want to be financially responsible. I hope that she will get along with my kids, so I should get along with hers. I want her to treat my children like they were her own." His mind was working around how close he wanted this stranger to be to his kids, but he wanted her very close. She would be their mother, after all.

"Did you answer the question or talk in a circle?" she asked, tilting her head slightly.

"I will support the twins, but what about the dad?" He did not want to deal with a dad in the picture; he already had enough to deal with from his kids' moms.

"The dad is a non-issue; he will never know about the babies," she stated firmly.

"Anything else?"

"Length of marriage. Would two years work? Granted that it could be longer if you're still working on the Chicago move. Those things might take time." She was still tapping away on the conference table.

"Two years would suffice. I was thinking five hundred grand for every year we are married. After that, the divorce would have to be completely uncontested, or no money would be given." He had been thinking about that, the divorce.

"I think that's doable, but she would like you to not sleep around. It's only two years, after all." Her fingers stilled as she bit hard on her bottom lip after she said it.

"Am I going to sleep with her?" he asked with a smile, seeing if Lucy would blush again.

"I don't know if you'd want to. She's pregnant and will be having two babies in that time, but she doesn't want you to act like you have been since I've known you. Her family is very protective, and she doesn't want them to know of this arrangement. She would like them to think the marriage is real and that it just ends because some do." She was tapping her fingers again.

"So, we'll be faking it. Big wedding and everything also?" He hadn't thought about the wedding part. He had been concentrating so hard on the marriage that he forgot about the wedding.

"No, just something small, like a courthouse or in the yard. Anything so that her mom could see her get married…. She probably won't again." Her fingers stopped moving and curled in tight fists on the table.

"I can do a small wedding for her mom. Very okay with that. Anything else?" he asked.

"Would she work or be home at this point, since your kids are at their moms' and school, there isn't much to do at home? What about after the babies are born?" she asked. So far, she had written nothing down, but he knew she would remember all of it and be able to tell the woman everything.

"I would say it's up to her. If she wants to work, she can, or she can quit or wait until the babies come. I'm flexible," he replied. This was going way better than he had ever thought. Lucy was a very good negotiator.

"Thank you for answering everything. That was all I had." She frowned and wrinkled her brow as she stared at her hand, which were tapping again. It was almost as if they were not a part of her body by the way she was analyzing them.

"Do I get to find out who it is tonight, or do you have to talk to her again? Have you talked to her?" He found himself unable to stop grinning and almost grabbed her hands in excitement. Even if he didn't know yet who she had found, she had found someone.

"I don't have to talk to her. I already know that she will do it if you're willing," she said as her hands slipped off the table.

"Do I get to know?" Leo tried not to chuckle. She was so fucking nervous it was almost cute.

"It's me," she said quietly, almost too quietly.

He stopped cold. He must have misheard her. "You're married."

She shook her head. "No, I'm not," she stated firmly, her secretary voice in action.

"But Mr. Lovely picks you up almost every day," he pointed out, hoping this was not a joke, because he suddenly wanted to be married to Lucy.

Lucy seemed confused. "Harrison? He's married to Sera, who lives down the street from me. We ride together." She shook her head.

Leo leaned forward. "Cliff? Who is Cliff?" he asked, needing to know everything.

"My friend, but he's now married to my sister." She shrugged as if he didn't mean anything to her.

"Your maiden name is Montgomery." He leaned back. She couldn't explain this one away.

Lucy's brow shot up. "My middle name has always been Montgomery. I was named after Lucy Maud Montgomery. She's an author of children's books." He had no idea who she was talking about.

"Why do you want to marry me?" he asked in disbelief.

Her hands were on her lap under the table, but he knew they were moving. "I am pregnant with twins and have no idea how to make that work on my own. I need help, and the father is nothing. In two years, the babies will have been born, we will divorce, and I will have some money saved up to take care of them. I don't need child support; I'll be fine. I'm just struggling right now. Once I am past that, I'll be fine."

"And we have to fool your family into thinking we're in love? Do they know about the babies?" he asked.

"Not yet, but nobody will care that they're not yours. They will care, however, that I married someone not for love," she said, looking back up at him.

"How are you going to explain us to them? That we fell in love at the office?" He didn't think that sounded too bad. That sort of thing happened all the time.

"I was thinking that I would say something happened when I brought your kids home both times. That we suddenly clicked. That we went from nothing to 'can't keep our hands off each other.' They'll get that."

"What if I really *can't* keep my hands off of you?" He was sure he wasn't going to make it two years with her in his house, pregnant or not.

Her face turned crimson at his words. "I-I don't know. I can't say it will or will not happen, just that it's a possibility."

"I have two questions for you then." He grinned at her, but clearly, she was still not sure about the entire thing.

"Okay." She tapped her fingers.

"How soon can we get this done, and do you want the finder's fee in cash or in your bank account?" He reached out and stopped her hand from tapping on the table.

"I ... I'm ready whenever you are. Just send the money to the bank," she replied, waiting for him to laugh at her.

"I think next week, midweek, or will that not work for you?"

"I can make that work." She smiled for the first time.

"Anything else?"

"Should I keep calling you Mr. Montgomery in the office or Leo? I want to stay working until I can't anymore," she said, surprising him. He had forgotten he would need a new secretary now.

"Leo, please. When did you want to move in?" The questions were suddenly never-ending, and he was enjoying his time with her.

She looked thoughtful. "After the wedding. No need to jump the gun."

"When do you want me to meet your family? I would like you to meet the girls soon, or at least all the girls together since you've met them all but Alexis recently. And I don't know if Aubrey even remembers you," he admitted. Aubrey hadn't said anything about her new friend since that night, it seemed she might have been too drunk to even remember Lucy.

"I don't know. I could be available this week sometime to meet the kids." She was tapping again, very quickly.

"How about tomorrow?" Leo suppressed a laugh as he straightened his tie. This plan was working out perfectly. His heartrate increased as he realized he was getting the wife he wanted sooner than he'd expected. Suddenly he was far more nervous about the entire situation. Now he wasn't going to marry some faceless woman, he was marrying Lucy. He didn't want to mess this up with Lucy.

"Then you're spending the night, and you can meet them the awkward Lovely way: the morning after. It works best, and they'll be completely into finding a man in the house. And then they'll buy that we're in love and getting married." She bit her lip as if she was starting to doubt it would work.

"How many live in the house?" he asked. It wasn't his favorite plan, even if it involved a night with his new fiancé.

"Just Agatha, but the morning will bring everyone home for breakfast. It's tradition," she rubbed the back of her neck as her eyes darted around the room.

"Agatha?" Leaning towards her, he hoped she wasn't having second thoughts.

"My sister. Meet you at my place tonight, around 10 p.m.?"

"Sure, that will be perfect." Well, not perfect. Perfect would be at *his* place.

But this was her plan, so he would go along with it. He just hoped it turned out like she was planning.

CHAPTER ELEVEN

Maybe this wasn't such a good idea, Lucy thought as she sat on the front step, waiting for her boss to show up to spend the night with her. Shaking her head, she tried to get "boss" out of it; he was Leo, and they were in love. Okay, maybe it was a stretch that they were in love or even lust, but tomorrow morning, she had to make it look real.

When she had come up with the idea, she had forgotten the one major event of this plan: him spending the night ... in her bed. It was going to be super uncomfortable.

A big pickup pulled up in front of the house, and Lucy realized she should have moved one of the vehicles that usually lived in front of her place. Agatha and her Jeeps were there, and Harper's old Jeep was there as well. Kane had bought her a Land Rover months before.

Lucy watched him park in front of the house next door and climb out of the cab and walk towards her place. Standing up as he approached, she saw he was in jeans and a black leather jacket, which was open to reveal a white T-shirt. Even his work boots made him look different than in the office. He was so fucking sexy she couldn't handle it.

She suddenly wished she hadn't worn black leggings and an oversized orange sweatshirt. Happily, the shirt only had the word "UM" on it, which meant nothing, but it was cute and large.

"Are you ready for this?" he asked with a smile as he walked up the steps to her.

"Ready as I will ever be." She tried to fake a smile but didn't really pull it off.

"Nice house. Is it yours?" he asked as she opened the door to let him inside.

"No, it's my parents, but Mom lives down the block now since she's remarried." She watched him take off his boots and jacket.

He glanced at her. "And your dad?"

"I have no idea. Haven't seen him in years." Bradford Lovely was just a name on forms now, nobody she could even recognize. It had been fifteen years since she had set eyes on him.

Her real mom was the same, just a name. Though she could get in contact with her, she didn't. None of her sisters did, either. Only Buzz and Harper had seen her and talked to her in the last two decades. From that, she knew the woman still didn't want anything to do with her five daughters, and now, she didn't want anything to do with the two she had raised after leaving the Lovelys. Lucy didn't let it bother her. She had a perfect mom and didn't need the old one.

"It's still a very nice house," he said, following her as she led him through it.

"This is the living room." She pointed out, and then to the kitchen. "Kitchen."

"Wow, this is nice." He looked around at the recently redone room. It had professional-grade everything, but it wasn't used much anymore. For years she and Harper had saved every spare dollar to make this room into what it was now.

"My sister is a caterer." She almost stumbled on the words, "so we have a professional kitchen. But she has one at her house now, so this is just a backup."

"A caterer? That must be nice," he said, looking at the room still.

"It is. She's a chef." Not adding that Lucy herself wasn't or how disappointed her sister was in her about it.

"My bedroom is upstairs."

"And your sister's also?" Leo asked as he followed her.

"No, hers is on the third floor. I'm alone on the second," she said as they made it to the top of the stairs.

"That's nice." He looked down the hallway.

Stopping at the stairway to the next level, she hollered up. "Goodnight, Agatha!"

"Goodnight, Lucy, have fun!" her little sister called down to them.

Across the hallway, she opened the door to the master bedroom. It was small, but it had the coveted attached bathroom. When Sera had actually moved out, there should have been a battle over the room, but so many sisters had moved out by then that it hadn't mattered.

"Does she know?" Leo asked as she shut the door behind them.

"It's after 10 p.m., and you are just getting here. She knows you're staying." Lucy cringed at how it sounded and wished she were a bit more embarrassed about it than she was.

"Can I say that I feel too old to spend the night in a girl's bedroom?" He grinned at her.

"Would it help if I said it was my mom's bedroom not that long ago?" She couldn't resist making him more uncomfortable.

"So, we're sleeping in your mom's bed?" He looked at it skeptically.

She looked at it also. "Yep. There are five other bedrooms on this floor if you want to stay in one of those."

"Where are you staying?"

"This is my room, so here."

"Then I'll sleep in your mom's bed as well."

"I'm going to get changed. I don't stay up late anymore." Lucy instantly regretted admitting that. She sounded like an old woman ... or just a pregnant one.

Going into the tiny adjoining bathroom, she brushed her teeth and wondered what Leo was thinking out there in her room. It had very little personality; she hadn't been there that long. Though she had put out a few knickknacks and gotten a new bedspread, it looked mostly the same as when her mom was there.

After changing into an oversized T-shirt, she took a deep breath and headed out to spend the night with her boss ... fiancé. It was odd that she was nervous since she'd had more than one one-night stand in her life, but she was always drunk when she did. Always.

Leo was sitting on the bed in just red boxers and a white T-shirt when she walked out of the bathroom. He looked gorgeous, just sitting there staring at the wall beside the bed. For a moment, she wondered if she would be able to keep her hands off of him when the lights went out. Her fingers itched to touch every muscle that had been hidden from her for so long.

She smiled at the drawing on the wall. "Agatha and Violet did that when Mom lived here. I hate to paint over it."

"Some are really good. It reminds me of a book I've read to the girls." He pointed at a deer.

"Agatha is an amazing artist; she just hasn't found a way to make money at it yet. She will one day." Lucy walked past him and around the bed to the other side.

"She is. Are you an artist?" He turned to her and watched her slide under the covers.

"No, I'm just a flounderer. I haven't found anything I'm good at yet. I don't think I ever will." She set her phone on the charger on the nightstand, not paying attention to him.

"Really? You're an amazing secretary. Your memory is outstanding." He slid under the covers next to her.

"Just a byproduct of being stupid, Leo. Nothing to be impressed with." She rolled away from him and shut the light off on the bedside table.

"You are not stupid. I don't even know why you would think that," he said. When she didn't answer, he asked, "How far along are you?"

Lucy rolled onto her back and looking at the ceiling. "Five months."

"And you're not showing?" He had turned to her in the darkness and was now propped up on an elbow.

"I am a little, but the nurse said I'm small," she admitted. It was weird talking about this with someone else.

"You are. Stacy was in maternity clothes by the time she was two months along, and Kelly, well, she didn't show as much as Stacy did." She felt him shrug in the dark.

"Stacy just likes to complain," Lucy replied and froze, realizing what she had just said out loud. "Sorry, I didn't mean that."

"Yes, you did, and you're right. She likes to complain." He agreed, and Lucy could tell he was grinning at her. She had always wondered if he saw Stacy the same way Lucy did, now that they were not married.

"I've always liked Kelly better, but her kids are older, and the divorce isn't as fresh for her." Lucy had analyzed it before. Why, she didn't know, because it hadn't affected her at all. But she had just the same.

"Kelly's always been more laid back than Stacy. We get along better, too," Leo said.

"Goodnight, Leo," she mumbled, not really wanting to talk about his exes.

"Goodnight, Lucy."

He rolled away from her, but she could still feel his warm body. The bed was small for two people who were trying not to touch each other in the dark.

CHAPTER TWELVE

It was almost 5 a.m. when Leo rolled off the sliver bed. Lucy was lying in the middle on her back, and her arms were above her head with her elbows sticking out. So, in the spot his head was supposed to be.

Opening his eyes in the dim light, he watched her sleep. Her breathing was even, and she wasn't making any noise. She wasn't moving at all. He had never seen her still; she was always fidgety.

Last night he had known she was asleep when her foot had stopped twitching. When Lucy was awake, something was always moving.

Looking at her stomach, he couldn't believe she was pregnant with twins. Her pregnancy was halfway over, and she wasn't even really showing. Just a small baby bump that was visible when you knew to look for it.

Reaching over, he rested his hand on her solid stomach. The thin cover didn't hide that it was hard and rounded. Not wanting to wake her, he pulled his hand away and just went back to watching her sleep.

As he watched, she rolled away from him onto her side and sat up. Without a word, she got up and walked around the bed and went into the attached bathroom.

A few minutes later, she came out, and her dark hair was brushed and put into a ponytail. She looked awake. Going to her dresser, she pulled out leggings and a sweatshirt and tossed them on the bed.

"Harper and Buzz are here already," she said and pulled on her leggings, giving him a glimpse of the lacy blue panties her T-shirt had hidden from him.

He didn't hear anything. "How do you know?"

Lucy pulled the orange sweatshirt over her head. "The mixer is on, and Buzz rides with her."

"How do you know?" he asked again, sitting up. He still couldn't hear anything going on downstairs.

"You can't hear the mixer? You must be old, losing your hearing," she joked with a grin.

"Thanks, but I don't hear it. Should I come down now?" he asked, realizing he didn't know the plan beyond last night.

She thought for a moment. "No, give it a half an hour or so and try to sneak out."

"What if I succeed?" he asked, turning to get out of bed.

"You won't—they'll be watching for you. Just take a shower or something." She shrugged.

Without another word, she walked out of the room and shut the door. Now he was starting to doubt her plan. Getting caught in a woman's bed by her family seemed off. Sure, she was just under thirty, but he was just under forty, and it felt wrong.

Taking her advice, he took a shower. Everything in the tiny bathroom smelled like her, from the shampoo to the body wash he used. As he pulled on his jeans, he smelled just like her. It wasn't a bad thing, but he liked it better on her than him.

As he combed his hair with her brush, he decided the best way to show her family they were in love was to kiss her the moment he saw her. It would oddly be their first kiss, and it would take place in front of them all, whoever they all were. So, no sneaking out at all for him.

After forty-five minutes, he headed down to prove to Lucy's family that they were in love—so in love that they were going to get married in less than a week.

At the bottom of the stairs, he saw her with her ponytail, leaning against the kitchen door frame. While he was showering, she had changed into jeans and a red T-shirt, but he knew that ass anywhere.

With a grin and a skip in his step, he grabbed her and spun her to face him. Her face showed complete surprise as his lips claimed hers. He had been thinking about kissing her for months now, but the reality of it was a disappointment. Though her lips were warm and soft, they were not kissing him back, and it just felt weird. None of the attraction he had felt for her for months was there.

With force, she pushed away from him and actually wiped her face with the back of her hand. He felt incredibly confused.

"You missed, lover boy. The one you want is over there," a dark-haired woman on a stool nearest him said and pointed at the table.

Lucy was sitting there in the same orange sweatshirt she had put on in front of him. Leo turned to the woman he kissed and then back to Lucy at the table. He just stared at them.

"I have missed this since Maby got married! When was the last time a man kissed the wrong twin the morning after?" A redhead said with a hearty laugh.

"We do not look alike, and do not tell Cliff," Lucy's twin said and wiped her lips again.

"Cliff loves it when you two play each other." A blonde who was sitting next to the black-haired woman said.

"Not kissing others!" the woman argued.

Lucy got up and said, "She's right; we don't look alike."

Both were lying to him. He was having a hard time telling them apart unless he looked at their shirts, and they looked nothing like anyone else in the room.

"Leo Montgomery," Lucy said, "The redhead is Bea. I look like her. The blonde one cooking is Harper, and Mabel looks way more like her than me. Agatha has black hair and a black soul to match. Sera, my mom, is eating a pork chop as if she hasn't eaten in weeks."

Everyone waved at him as Lucy said their names. Nobody made it seem odd he just came down the stairs or just kissed the wrong person, nor that the woman she just called mom wasn't a decade older than she was.

"Violet is the little one, and Emma is the sulking teen." She finished with the introductions. The last three kind of resembled each other.

"Hello." He didn't know what else to say.

"Hi, Leo," Harper replied from behind the counter. "Do you want a muffin or pork chops?"

"Muffin," was all he could say as the group studied him.

With a knowing smile, Bea handed him a plate with a muffin on it. "So, Leo, what do you do?"

"He's her boss." Mabel, the twin, informed her sister.

"Boss sex! It has been a while for that one, hasn't it, Harper?" Agatha shot at her sister, who was pulling something from the oven.

"Shut up, Agatha!" the blonde said from in the oven.

"You and Lucy should talk a little about that one." Bea laughed as her sister stood up and scowled at them all.

Leo took his muffin and sat at the table across from the sullen teen, just like at home. He let the conversation go on around him. Lucy sat down next to him, but she wasn't eating anything. Maybe she had already eaten.

He was starting to worry that Lucy wasn't liking being teased. It worried him that her sisters weren't noticing that she wasn't liking it. So far, she had not joined in on any of it. Even the smile she had on her face when he came into the room was completely gone.

"Quit teasing Harper, girls," Sera scolded the others. "Can I have another pork chop, Harper?"

"Really, Sera?" Bea demanded from beside her.

"Hey, I'm hungry and pregnant. I deserve another serving," Sera replied to the redhead as another plate was handed over to her.

"So am I, but I'm restrained," Bea stated, pushing her empty plate away from her.

Leo looked at the two women who were not even showing one bit yet, then back at Lucy, who wasn't showing either. Maybe she wasn't eating, and that was why she stayed thin. Either way, she was clearly not telling them today she was pregnant, even though now was the perfect time. Lucy remained silent beside him with her toes tapping, but nobody noticed.

Sera eyed Bea. "Just wait, Buzzy. It's coming."

"Did you want a muffin, Lucy?" he asked quietly, and her brown eyes swung back to him.

"No, I'm fine. Thanks." She put her hands on the table and started tapping against the wood.

"I think you need something," Leo commented, hoping only she could hear.

"Don't worry, Leo. Lucy no longer eats what I make. Agatha says she eats later in the morning." Harper tossed something in the sink that made a loud clatter.

"It's not like that, Harper. I'm just not hungry in the mornings like I used to be," Lucy told her sister.

"You mean you won't eat what I make anymore. You know I get up early to bring food over here, and you haven't made anything in months."

"I know, I just don't feel like making anything." The tapping had stopped, and he could tell she was looking beyond her sister, not at her sister.

"Let her be, Harper. She has company," Mabel said from the counter. Her eyes were definitely giving Harper a warning.

"Company? Really, Luce, are you going to start that again?" The blonde wasn't letting up today as she rounded the counter for the first time.

"I'm not going to sit here and take this," Lucy said, getting up and heading towards the door to leave the kitchen.

As Lucy rushed out of the room, Harper ran at her and slammed her into the wall behind them. It was so unexpected and quick that Leo could do nothing but watch it happen. Lucy's head hit the wall, and she slid down it under the weight of her sister, who then punched her in the back before Agatha and Mabel pulled her off.

Rushing to Lucy's side, he touched her cheeks, checking for damage, even though he knew the most damage could be with the babies. He ran his hands over her body just in case, relieved when he felt nothing that resembled a broken bone. Relief flooded him that she was outwardly okay.

"Lucy, are you okay?" he asked gruffly, using his body to block her from her sisters, glad that nobody else touched her because he didn't know what they would do to her. Woman or not, he wasn't letting anything happen to her again this morning. From how the other sisters reacted, this wasn't a usual activity for them.

"My head hurts." Her voice quivered as she held it, not her stomach, which he was thankful for. Her worried eyes were focused on her belly.

Harper was no longer going to attack Lucy, so her sisters had let her go. She had taken a step closer to him and Lucy, but it seemed all the fight in her was gone.

Without thinking, he kissed Lucy's forehead and lifted her into his arms. To his surprise, she went willingly but kept holding her head.

Turning, he eyed the blonde and hissed at her, "If anything like that ever happens again, you won't be allowed anywhere near her. Do you understand me?"

"Who do you think you are? You have no control over who she sees!" Harper hissed right back at him holding her ground.

"In less than a week, she will be living in my house and will be my wife, so I have a lot of say in it. If you cannot control yourself, I will control you. Try me." He walked out of the room, Lucy's body was shaking as he carried her away from her family and those who claim to love her.

Yes, it was too much, but he never wanted to see Lucy get hurt again. Not by her sisters, not by anyone.

Carrying her up to her room, he knew someone was following, but he didn't know who. He hoped it wasn't Harper because he was still ready to pound her into a wall for what she had done.

After setting Lucy gently on the bed, he looked into her eyes to make sure there wasn't a concussion. Her eyes were clear. Then he ran his hands down her body. Nothing was broken, but he knew that because she would have already said. Her eyes watched what he was doing.

"Are you still okay?" He ran a hand over her head, the only thing she said was hurting.

"Yes, t-thank you." She sounded shaken.

"Sorry I yelled at your sister." He was enjoying being able to just touch her, her soft, smooth skin warm under his hands.

"I think you just told everyone we're getting married." She didn't take her eyes off of him, reminding him of his words. They hadn't discussed how they were going to tell everyone, but the cat was out of the bag.

"That he did," the woman behind them said softly.

"Sorry, Mom, I was going to tell you," Lucy said, looking away from him and to the woman by the door.

The woman walked farther into the room and hugged her daughter. He had been expecting anger, disappointment, or surprise. Instead, she ran a hand over the new bump on Lucy's head. "You told me now, Luce. When? We have so much to do."

"Wednesday," Lucy said meekly. Her mom seemed not to care that it was so soon; she just seemed excited about the event.

"Congratulations! Lovelys marry so quickly. Agatha will already be married before I know about it. I didn't think I had a long engagement at four months, but it seems it was a lifetime."

"Sorry, Mom, but when you find the one...." Lucy shrugged.

"Oh, I know all about finding the one. He seems to be a keeper," Sera winked at Leo. "He fought off Harper for you, but I don't think he will get everyone to stop fighting. Only last month it was Mabel who took you down, or did you take Mabel down?" Her mom ran a hand over her head again.

"I did. She was being snooty. I forgot to tell him about the fighting." She pushed her mom's hand away.

"Well, you better. Now about the wedding, we need to go dress shopping this morning." Sera got to her feet. Her excitement was far more than he had expected from anyone.

"Nope, we're going to tell his kids today about us getting married," Lucy replied.

"Kids?" Sera turned and looked at him as if he had them with him in the room.

"I have four girls," he said, wondering if their new stepmom would teach them to fight.

Sera smiled. "More girls. How old?"

"Nineteen, sixteen, ten, and eight."

"They're my kids' ages. Well, my biological kids; they are fifteen and eight," she said.

"Everything is overlapping, Mom. My step-kids will be older than your kids. When I am married they will be your grandkids," Lucy replied.

Sera laughed, and Leo wondered if she knew her daughter would have babies before she did. "Let it happen, Lucy. I'll set up for us to go shopping tomorrow. My favorite shop will open for us—I've spent some good money there over the last few months. Fuck, you're my fourth daughter to get married in under six months, not including me! I'll start planning."

With a kiss on her daughter's head and punch in his arm, she left the room, pulling her phone from her pocket.

"Most of those women are married?" he asked when they were alone.

"Yes, just Agatha is single." She felt her stomach for the first time now that they were alone.

He went back to her. "Are you hurting? The babies?"

"No, they seem to be fine." She kept touching them, her brows furrowed.

"Tell me if anything feels wrong." He sat down next to her and pulled her to him. "I do not want to see your sister do that again. Once the babies are born, do what you want, but until then, it has to stop."

"I've been avoiding it. Mabel is easy and lets me win all the time." He felt her shrug.

They stayed in her room until Agatha stopped by and said everyone was gone.

"Harper is pissed at your man friend, but she married an ass, so she may not be the best judge of character." Agatha grinned at her own joke.

"Kaine's fine now. Thanks for telling me, Agatha," Lucy said.

"Sure, don't let Harper bait you. She's quick when she wants to be." Agatha leaned against the door frame. "If I didn't know better, I would think you set the entire thing up. Every one of them are going home wondering if their man would carry them away from a battle."

"Shut up, Agatha," Lucy growled at her.

"Just saying, and thanks for another day wasted in the fucking bridal shop. If I thought I would ever get married, I would pick up something for me while we're there so that I never have to go back. But with you married, I shouldn't have to go back until Emma, and she had better have some years before that happens." Agatha put her hands together like she was praying.

"You'll be fine, Ag. I know you secretly love taffeta," Lucy teased her. So far today, she hadn't teased anyone.

"Fuck you, Luce, and the man who is making this wedding possible." Agatha turned to leave but then stopped. "But next time, I think you should have sex. It would be more believable for me if you had."

With that, she was gone. He could hear her footsteps going up to her room. Of all the sisters, she seemed to be the one with the most personality.

Leo kissed Lucy on the forehead and left. She had promised to call if she felt anything off, but he had to get home and get ready to introduce his kids to their future stepmother.

CHAPTER THIRTEEN

LUCY HAD ALWAYS BEEN good with kids and thought that she had Leo's youngest two wrapped around her finger after the previous week. But apparently, the older ones had convinced them that Lucy was bad news. Even Aubrey, who she had brought home weeks before, was not impressed she was dating her dad. So much for her never wanting Lucy to leave her.

Leo had met her at the door when she arrived. He had informed her that he had told the kids at lunch, and they were not excited about him getting married again. Oddly, she was starting to doubt wanting to be the third Mrs. Montgomery, but Sera had been told, and the woman was planning the wedding as they spoke.

Shutting the door after she got into the house, he stopped her by taking her hand.

"Lucy, I have something for you before we talk to the kids." He pulled her back to him but didn't let go of her hand.

"Okay." She looked at him in question. Were they giving gifts? Because if so, she had nothing. Maybe she should have brought wine or something, but only Leo could drink it, so it would have looked odd.

Leo reached into his jeans pocket, his sexy, tight jeans that made her mouth water when she saw him in them. Pulling out a ring, he slid it onto her hand. She almost choked when she looked at it. The ring was bigger than Mabel's, and Mabel had gotten a rock from Cliff.

"Leo, I can't take this." She shook his hand from hers and pulled the ring off.

"Yes, my fiancé would wear my ring," he replied, grabbing it away from her and slipping it back on her finger.

"Something smaller, maybe?" She looked at it again. It was very pretty, but not something she could wear on a day-to-day basis. Definitely not something she could cook in, but then again, she didn't cook much anymore.

"You get to keep it after," Leo stated, still holding her hand so that she didn't take it off.

"I don't want it. When it is over, I will leave it." She looked at it again, already missing it when she said goodbye to this life.

With the ring argument over, he let go of her hand and left the ring on through the formal introduction to the children and to the meal that she had been invited to.

Lucy wasn't letting some negative vibes from teenagers get in the way of her and food that night. Leo had ordered stuffed shells from a local restaurant. They were good, but once again, they were short on sauce and could use about a quarter more seasoning. Lucy was digging into her third shell by the time Leo had convinced the others to even try them.

"This is not something I eat, Dad," Addison stated and pushed away her plate.

"Have you even tried them before?" Leo asked his daughter.

"Nope, but I know I won't like them," Addison confirmed.

"Me either," Amelia stated from beside her sister. The two blondes were in complete agreement about the meal. They were acting exactly like they had in Leo's office not so long ago. It had taken hours for them to warm up then, and Lucy wasn't expecting anything less now.

"What don't you like about them?" Lucy asked the pair. So far, the older ones hadn't voiced their hatred of the food, but they weren't eating either.

"I don't even know what's in them." Addison looked at the lonely shell that on her plate.

"Tomato sauce, sausage, ground beef, two or three cheeses, and seasoning all stuffed into a shell, and more sauce is added." Lucy shrugged. It was an easy dish, and she had always loved when they served them while catering.

"Gross," Alexis pushed her plate away from her and rolled her eyes. It was the first thing she had said during the meal.

"What's gross about it? It's spaghetti with less mess," Lucy told her.

"No, it's gross," Alexis stated stubbornly. She narrowed her eyes at Lucy.

It seemed all three of her sisters agreed with her assessment. Oddly, this was a go-to meal at the Lovely house. Everyone ate it and loved it. Add garlic bread, and they were in hog heaven. Watching Alexis poke her shell with a fork, Lucy decided to do what her step-mother would do in this situation.

Having just added two more shells onto her plate, she stuck her fork in the middle of the biggest one and flung it at Leo's second daughter. The shell hit her on the chin and rolled down her black T-shirt onto her lap. Her blue eyes looked at Lucy in shock at what had just happened.

Lucy stabbed the next one and flung it at Addison, who had called the shells gross. Addison was ready for it and tried to catch it in one hand, but it fell apart mid-air, flinging sauce and meat all over her face and cat T-shirt. She managed to fling back the bits that remained on her hands, but the kid was smiling as she did it, and Lucy hoped that she got some in her mouth so that she knew how good it was.

This time, Lucy had to dig in the pan to fling one at Aubrey before Alexis threw back the one that had landed on her lap. Aubrey had been watching her sister and missed the fact that she was under attack until it hit her face. Both shells hit Lucy, one after another, and she couldn't stop them from hitting her white shirt and face, realizing only as the sauce spattered across her chest that she hadn't dressed for a food fight.

Grinning at her enemies, she went for another and quickly threw it at Amelia, who had been safe until then. Then she sent one back to Alexis, who was suddenly aware of the battle and sent it lobbing back at Lucy.

By the time Lucy's pan was empty, the room was covered in sauce, and so were the four girls. Leo had come away with nothing on him; his girls were good at aiming.

Turning to the man she was going to marry, she was a bit disappointed he had not participated in the battle. But then again, she wondered what side he would have been on. His kids or hers?

He was not smiling. In fact, he looked mad at what she had done, which was childish. But it had gotten all the kids to loosen up and have a little fun even when they were pissed at their dad.

"Everyone, upstairs and shower. Try not to get anything on the floor," Leo stated, getting up from the table.

"Leave your clothes on the floor in the bathrooms. I'll take care of them," Lucy added. It wasn't the first time she had to take red sauce out of some clothes.

As the girls got up, they were a little nervous because their dad sounded mad. Lucy bit her lip as she worried that she maybe went a little too far, then took it over the edge.

With the last half-shell that had landed on her lap, she grabbed it and threw it at the man who she was supposed to marry in a few days—a man who was probably thinking about grounding her right now.

The shell hit him in the heart, though it was hard to tell with his red shirt. His eyes snapped down at the shell falling to the ground, then at her. The girls starting laughed at him and his disbelief at what had happened.

He smiled at them and gave a fake laugh in return. Even Lucy knew it was fake.

Yup, too far.

Once the girls were out of the room, she got up from her chair and stood by the table, ready to be yelled at. Maybe one day she would look back and laugh at her two-day engagement to her boss.

"Did you really start a food fight with my kids?" he asked as he rounded the table back to her.

"Yes, they needed loosening up," she explained. It sounded lame even to her, but it was the truth.

"Did you throw food at me?" he demanded, pointing at the wet red spot on his otherwise perfect shirt.

"No, that was someone else." She grinned, as if he would buy that.

"I would throw some at you if there were any more left." His eyes slid down her body. "Or if you weren't completely covered in it already."

Without thinking, she grinned and ran her hands over his shirt, her hands covered in red sauce and little bits of meat and shells. "Like *that*?"

Too late, he grabbed her hands and pushed them above her head, away from him. He was suddenly close to her, too close. Whether his blue eyes were looking at her or the sauce on her face, she didn't know. But she couldn't look away from him.

"I would ground you if you weren't so fucking cute right now," he stated huskily as his lips lowered to hers.

He tasted of red sauce. He wasn't covered in the stuff, so it must have been on her lips. The taste alone made her want more of him. Her tongue darted out to taste his lips, only to meet his doing the same.

Tilting her head, his hands let go of hers and pulled her closer to him.

With her arms free, she was able to push out of his arms. Not that she wanted to, but she needed to. At this point, she didn't need to fall for him. That wasn't what their relationship was about.

To her surprise, he let her go as she looked around the room. "I have to clean this."

"I'll clean up. You have to take a shower also." He ran a finger over her cheek and licked the sauce from it.

"I guess I might have lost," she admitted with a smile, pushing all thought of the kiss from her mind.

"Four against one, you were going to lose." He grabbed her hand and pulled her from the dining room.

She let her competitive side show. "I was ahead for a little while."

Pulling her up the stairs, he replied, "For two shells, then you were fighting a losing battle."

"I'll win next time."

"Next time?" He towed her into the master suite that made her bedroom look like an efficiency apartment.

"Figure of speech." She grinned as he showed her the bathroom.

"Next time, you're cleaning the dining room." He let go of her hand.

"Next time, you will be involved," she replied, looking at the shower, his shower.

"I'll go find you something to wear." He walked out of the bathroom, shutting the door softly behind him.

Patting herself on the back for not inviting him to shower with her, she admitted staying out of Leo's bed for two years was going to be impossible. After that kiss, it was all she could think about. And sadly, she would think about him whenever she tasted red sauce. It was one of her favorites, but now it would be a constant reminder of that kiss.

CHAPTER FOURTEEN

AFTER FINDING Lucy clothes to wear, Leo cleaned the dining room as well as he could. His maid would have to take care of the rest in the morning. Sauce was everywhere, but as he cleaned, he couldn't get mad at Lucy for what she did. She had made his kids laugh.

Also, it had gotten him a first kiss to remember: her covered in red sauce and grinning from ear to ear as she lied about throwing food at him. Then he had kissed those lips he had been dreaming of and, unlike with kissing her sister, it had been perfect.

Soon the kids would come down from their showers in pajamas. It was a ritual that they have a movie night if they were all together on the weekends. With the kids' rotating schedules, he tried to make it special when all four were in the house, knowing that the older they got, the rarer it was going to be to have them together.

Aubrey was the first one down the stairs, and her eyes were searching the area for something. Lucy, he assumed.

"Where is your girlfriend, Dad?"

"Fiancé, Aubrey, and she's taking a shower. You girls got her dirty," he reminded her. Lucy had been dirtier than any of the other kids.

Aubrey tried to shift the blame away from herself. "She started it, you know. If anyone is going to get in trouble, she is."

"Nobody is in trouble. I hope that you girls just remember to thank Lucy for getting you out of actually eating something you didn't want to."

"I think she's only looking out for herself." Aubrey leaned against the wall. "She's only after you for your money."

"Nope. She's signing a prenup," he told her. She was old enough to understand a lot of stuff.

"She's closer to my age than yours." Aubrey's jaw was set.

Leo could tell she was trying to not like Lucy but wasn't succeeding. He knew exactly how she was feeling. Lucy was hard to resist.

"I think she's right between us. Ten years from us both." Smiling at her, he was reminded he needed to ask Lucy when her birthday was.

"She seems nicer than Stacy, but that isn't hard," Aubrey stated, watching the stairs, not wanting her little sisters to hear her say it.

"Why?"

"Why what?"

"Why do you think she's nicer than Stacy?"

"Because she and her sisters helped me when Kevin abandoned me drunk in a strange bar," Aubrey said, something she hadn't talked about since that night. He had thought she had blacked out on it all.

"Which will never happen again, right?" He gave her the look, the one he had been mastering since she had been born.

She shrugged. "I ran into him a few days ago. He was very different when I was sober. I'm over him."

"Good. He's over thirty," he said, reminding her of the age differences she had just pointed out for him.

She grinned at his response. "And your girlfriend's ex. Or at least that's what her sisters said, one of which looks just like her."

"That would be Mabel—they're twins. I met her family this morning." It felt like weeks ago and not just a few hours. They had gone from this all being a plan to being in the middle of it within hours.

"Why are you getting married so quickly? You've known her for a long time, so why suddenly now?" Aubrey crooked an eyebrow at him, just like her mother did all the time. It was something he wouldn't tell her, that she was constantly reminding him of her mom.

"I fell in love with her and realized how much time we wasted, time where I could've had her in my life. Like tonight. How did I not know she was handy in a food fight?" Yes, he was laying it on thick, but Aubrey could see through him more than the other kids.

Not that it was all a lie; he did want her in his life, food fights and all. He was looking forward to learning more and more about her.

"Okay, Dad. I believe you," Aubrey said as the two little ones came running down the stairs. Leo knew she didn't actually believe him, but he hoped in time, they would be able to fool all the kids into thinking they were in love. Just like her family.

Though for the first time, he wondered if he was making a mistake, that his kids would fall in love with their new stepmom, and then they would divorce. He'd be breaking up another family and would have two more kids to keep connected with his girls. Or not, because they weren't really his. Could he raise someone else's kids?

Lucy was the last one down from showering. She had walked into the family room wearing cute little sweatpants that hugged her ass and his navy shirt that was way too large for her. Her hair was wet as it hung down her back. She smelled fresh and clean and plopped down beside him.

The girls had started an older movie, and Lucy commented that she liked their pick as she snuggled in closer to him. But within minutes, she was sleeping. He could tell because her hand quit tapping on his leg. He didn't think she'd realized she'd been doing it.

She was still sleeping when he had silently sent the girls to bed, then followed them to help the younger two get ready, read to them, and make sure they were sleeping. He knew he should've woken Lucy up in case she wanted to go home, but instead, he carried her to his bedroom and slid her under the covers. When she didn't wake up, he slipped out of his clothes down to his boxers and slid in beside her. She only sighed when he pulled her into his arms.

It was the second night they had slept together, and so far, he was enjoying their engagement. She wasn't the ice queen he had thought she was. In fact, he couldn't remember why he had ever thought that in the first place.

CHAPTER FIFTEEN

Since she was up at 4 a.m., she decided to head home after taking time to gather up all the stained clothes and make a batch of muffins that she left for them to bake when they got up. Today she had to go dress shopping with her mom and sisters, and she was not looking forward to it.

After four times into the shop, she knew what to expect, and it was going to take all day. Nobody would be satisfied until she had tried on at least twelve dresses, and then they would pick the first one.

The house was empty when she got there, but people would soon be arriving, so she headed up to her room. After slipping off the green shirt Leo had given her to wear, she missed his scent immediately. Without thinking, she sniffed the balled-up shirt before tossing it into the laundry. She was losing it.

Another night she had slept beside him, but this time he was everywhere. His smell surrounded her, and she had woken up in his arms. Not a bad way to wake up.

When she had decided to become his wife, she had also decided to not sleep with him. Within a few weeks, he would cheat, and she would be just another notch on his headboard, and be there watching it happen while helping him raise his kids.

When she had been cheated on before, she had been able to walk away from the relationship, but this time she had to stay for two years. Then she would have to watch the parade of women in his life, and there was nothing she could do about it. If they didn't sleep together, she hoped it wouldn't be as bad.

After changing into leggings and a gray sweatshirt, she headed down to pretreat all the stains she had caused the day before. But it was worth it to see those kids laughing and teasing each other. It was something she was sure they missed. They didn't spend all that much time together, and Aubrey was already an adult.

With everything waiting to go in the washer in an hour or so, she headed upstairs to find Harper, Buzz, and Sera bringing food into the kitchen. Grabbing Buzz's load, the redhead smiled and went back for another. They always brought more food than was needed.

Within minutes, Harper was getting things ready and had both ovens preheating. She didn't even turn around to ask, "No fiancé this morning?"

"No, I just got home a few minutes ago." Take that, Harper Hawthorn! No way was she saying she hadn't planned on staying overnight, although that might've worked in her favor also. She just couldn't say she fell asleep watching TV.

"Poor Agatha. She has to be in the house alone. Maybe she should get roommates," Sera said.

"She does not want roommates." Agatha walked into the room. Her hair was a mess, and she was still in her pajamas.

"But when Lucy moves out, you will be lonely," Buzz said.

"No, I won't. I'll be fine." Agatha sat down next to her mom.

"Maybe Lucy's man can move in," Harper said sarcastically.

"He already has a house and four kids. Agatha does not want that," Lucy told her.

"No, she doesn't. Keep your sex and kids away from me," Agatha said. "If nothing is ready, I'm going to take a shower."

The rest watched her go, and Sera asked, "So, are you going to keep working after you marry your boss?"

"Yes, I am. Maybe in a while, I'll see if there's anything else I want to do." It wasn't something she had recently thought of because all she really wanted to do was be a caterer. And only then with her sister.

"But you love being a personal assistant," Harper stated as if she were telling Lucy it was true. Like they had ever talked about it or talked at all since they quit working together.

"Yeah, I like it." She lied. She didn't want to go into how hard it actually was. She had enough emotions swirling around in her head, and she didn't need any more.

"I made a list of things that have to get done before the wedding." Sera slid an open little notebook her way.

Glancing down at it, she pushed it back at her stepmom. "You can take care of it."

"No, Lucy, it's your wedding. How does it look? Am I missing anything? It's been months since I've done one of these, but I think I can still plan one in my sleep." She pushed the notebook back at her.

Lucy picked it up and looked at the words. Nothing made any sense to her. In fact, she knew her mom had written it all in cursive, a language Lucy had never been able to decipher. Biting her lip, she just looked at the paper.

"I will be fine," she mumbled, still looking at the paper.

"Lucy, what's wrong?" Sera turned to her in concern.

"I can't read this." She tossed it on the table in anger as angry tears burned the back of her eyes.

"Of course, you can, Lucy. You have a diagnosis. You're better," Harper said, dropping her potholder on the counter.

"No, I'll never be better. I know what I have, but I'm still just as stupid as I always was." Pushing away from the counter, she rushed up to her room and slammed the door behind her.

Sitting on her bed, she looked out the window at the neighbor's gray house, letting the hot tears roll down her cheek. Her family had thought that since Lucy had a diagnosis, there was a magic switch that went off and made Lucy all better, that everything had changed when someone told her she had dyslexia. But in reality, nothing had changed. She was still reading at a second-grade level and would never progress beyond that. She had only gotten better and better at covering it up from others.

Her door opened behind her, but she didn't look up, "Are you okay, Lucy?"

"I'm fine," she mumbled to her mom and wiped away the tears.

"Can I come in?" Sera asked, but Lucy knew she was already in the bedroom.

"I'm fine," she repeated.

"You're not stupid, Lucy. You never were." Sera sat on the other side of the bed.

"Just different, right?. That's what they always called it. And I went to classes with all the other *different* kids. Mabel didn't, just me. Alone," Lucy said, letting the tears fall freely.

"Why didn't you tell me back then? I knew you were struggling, but I didn't know why."

"I didn't know why either. I just thought I was too dumb to figure it out and that everyone else was just better than me. Mabel knew how to read before we started school, but it never made sense to me. For a while, I thought Mom left because I wasn't smart enough. I thought I was to blame for her being gone." She admitted her secret, the one she had carried for longer than she liked to admit. Sometimes, she still felt that way.

Sera rubbed a hand up her back. "You know that's not true. Your mom left for whatever reason, but she was to blame for leaving, not one of you kids."

"I kept thinking that one day I would just get it, like magic. By the time you showed up, I had given up. I was in special education classes, and kids who were mentally challenged could learn to read, but I couldn't. Now it's too late, and I'll be like this forever. Forever the one making shirts with everything spelled wrong. The joke." She angrily wiped at the tears still clinging to her cheeks. She didn't want to talk about her faults.

"You're not a joke to any of us. We wear the shirts because *they* are the joke. At the heart of it, we wear them because we love them and you for making them."

"They're dumb," Lucy said, though she was wearing one even as they spoke. They both were.

"How do you do it at work?" Sera asked with interest.

"I have all the documents read to me by the computer. I have Leo's calendar memorized."

"What is he doing tomorrow at 3 p.m.?"

Wiping away her tears, she stated, "Marketing meeting from two to four. Before that is a lunch meeting at The Detail. I have it memorized for weeks." She shrugged. It had gotten easy to keep up with.

"But I text you all the time," Sera said.

"And I have them read to me. I speak to text back so that you don't know I can't read them. Everyone likes to text but me," she ended in a whisper.

"Do you want me to stop texting and leave voicemails instead? How can I make life better for you?" Sera asked.

"Just don't tell everyone. They don't need to know I'm as stupid as I am. I can't get smarter, but I can pretend," Lucy said.

"You are not stupid; you have a disability."

"Try telling that to a waiter when you have no idea what to order. Or the lady in the grocery store when you're trying to find the box that says, 'original flavor,' or your sister who … forget it." Lucy couldn't tell her that she knew that her sister had stopped wanting to spend time with her when she had found out. It was why Harper hated her now.

"They all love you, but they can't understand if you won't talk about it," Sera said.

"I haven't told Leo, so please don't." There was no need for him to know she was defective. Better he found out after it was too late.

"You should tell him. I can't believe he doesn't know already. But he won't care because it makes you who you are," Sera replied and gave her a big hug. "Come down when you're ready. And I talked to the girls—no fighting until after the wedding. I couldn't get any more time than that."

"Thanks. Leo isn't used to the battles." Lucy finally smiled. Leo would have to get used to it. She only hoped his kids didn't pick up on the habit, or she would stop liking it also.

"Hopefully, he doesn't mind the teasing because you five are very good at that. It's one of the things I miss the most about not living here."

"I miss you being here as well, and he'll have to get used to the Lovelys." She sighed, knowing he would only have to put up with it for two years. Then it would be over.

Within two hours, they walked into the tranquil bridal store that was usually closed on Sunday. But since no one could say no to her stepmom, and she had spent thousands in the store over the last few months, it was open for them.

As the manager looked through the rows of white dresses, Lucy was able to whisper to her that if she managed to find a great dress that hid that she was pregnant from her mom, she would pay her $500 under the table.

Two dresses in, she had the one. It wasn't her favorite, but it made her look gorgeous and hid the baby bump she wasn't ready to tell her mom about yet. So, the group was able to go out to lunch and have a good time, and nobody teased her about getting married quickly. Her mom must have talked to them that morning.

Though she had always loved the teasing and the roughhousing, she was tired of being in the center of it. Being reminded of every single mistake she has ever made was getting old. If she told them she was pregnant it would be just another thing. But she didn't want her babies to be thought of as another Lucy mess up. They were special if only to her.

CHAPTER SIXTEEN

WHEN STACY PICKED up the kids, he happily told her he was marrying his personal assistant. Her prejudice against people who work was showing when her only response was, "Why?" Only to be matched by an equally disgusted reply when he said they were in love. That hadn't even been the reason he had married her. Love had never even crossed his mind. It had been a short, hot affair that had ended with an unplanned pregnancy. Even now, he knew he had never loved her.

Still grumbling, she took the two little girls and left. Happily, they were talking about nothing but the woman Stacy was growing to hate. It was Lucy this, and Lucy that as they walked down the sidewalk. It was a good day.

One of the downsides of the day was that Lucy hadn't been in his bed that morning when he had woken up. Though he didn't know when she had left, she had left breakfast for him and his kids and had oddly taken all the stained clothes from the day before. He had decided they weren't worth the effort of cleaning.

Now he was just waiting for Kelly to show up and pick up the older kids. Though both could drive now, she still liked the ritual of picking them up—a big difference between his exes.

"Leo, I hear you're getting married." Her voice came from the doorway. She usually just let herself in, and today was no different.

"That I am, to the love of my life," he said with a grin. He and Kelly were friends now after all these years. Their marriage had been a mistake from the beginning, but their divorce had been almost perfect.

"I hope so. You deserve to find her. New personal assistant of yours? I like her." Kelly sat down across from him on the other couch.

"I like her too," he admitted the truth. Was he in love with her? No, he didn't believe in love after all these years.

"At least she's better than Stacy. I mean, Stacy would never bring your drunk kid home from a bar. She would've left her," Kelly said, and it was true.

"I've talked to Aubrey about that night. The guy she was with was over thirty." Leo was still relieved Lucy had been there for his kid.

"She says he's not," Kelly said, defending her daughter.

"Lucy says he is, and she dated him for a while." Leo hated to tell her. Lucy's business was not Kelly's.

"Your fiancé's ex is dating your kid?" Kelly's face was in shock.

"No, because my kid isn't dating him. He's *thirty*," Leo reminded her.

"I'll talk to her about it," Kelly replied, moving over to his side of that argument.

"She said yesterday she wasn't interested anymore, and I hope she was telling the truth. No need for her to end up with the wrong guy at nineteen." Leo grinned at her.

"Oh, it wasn't so bad, Leo. I got two great kids and a great ex-husband from the deal. But maybe I should have waited a few years."

"We made it work for a while."

"Until you started thinking like your dad, we were good," she agreed.

He frowned. "I do not think like my dad.".

"The minute he talked you in to working with him, you turned into a cheating workaholic." Kelly leaned back in her chair, waiting for him to defend his dad as he always did.

"He had a heart attack, Kelly." It had been the reason Leo had given up his dreams to follow his dad's path.

"And lived for another ten years." Kelly snorted. She never believed he'd had a real heart attack.

"Did you leave me because I cheated?" He needed to know because he didn't want his next marriage to end after two years. He was already wanting to be a part of his kids' lives.

"Yes, and no. You cheated more than once, but I divorced you because I didn't care anymore. I didn't want to waste my life with a man who I didn't care was sleeping around. I wanted one that I wanted in my bed." They had always had issues in the bedroom—there was too much of a past between them, which was why they were better as friends now.

"And you found him," Leo said of Bruce, her second husband, the cop. They had been married for a decade now.

"I did. But I want you to find yours. I want this one to work," Kelly said, and he could tell she meant it.

"Me too. Wedding's on Wednesday if you want to come."

"Tell me about her. I know the personal assistant stuff."

"She's smart and outgoing. I met her sisters and stepmom, which was interesting. And last night, she started a food fight with the girls. She lost." He grinned at the memory of her covered in red sauce and not even caring.

"What's her name?" Kelly pulled out her phone.

"Lucy Lovely, you know that." He leaned back in his chair. Kelly wouldn't find a thing on this woman.

"Lucy Lovely." Kelly tapped. Turning the phone to him, she asked, "Does she look like that?"

Leo took the phone from her and looked at his fiancé's face in a wedding announcement, a wedding that took place not six months before, based on the write-up. He nodded to his ex; it was her.

Kelly took the phone back and read, "Mabel Lucie Lovely marries Clifton Scott V in a late summer wedding."

"Her twin is named Mabel," Leo told her. If he hadn't seen her twin the day before, he wouldn't believe that she wasn't in that picture.

"Mabel Lucie and Lucy?" Kelly raised an eyebrow in question.

"Lucy Maud." Leo grinned. He had no idea why her parents would name their twins that. He wondered for a second what they would name their boys.

Kelly looked at the article again. "Oh, look. Lucy Lovely was maid of honor."

"See."

"Do you know who Clifton Scott V is, Leo?" Kelly pointed at her phone screen, even if he couldn't see it.

"Nope." He raised his hand in defeat.

"Billionaire whose family put up most of the money for the new library last fall."

"So, she married well." Leo shrugged.

"She was also maid of honor for Harper Lovely, who married Kaine Hawthorn." Kelly pointed to her phone. "Another billionaire in this town."

Which was why her knowing Bex Carter wasn't a big deal. She knew the owner of Hawthorn International.

"Another sister married well."

"And she was a bridesmaid for Beatrix Lovely, who married Jonas Raiden. Three for three, Leo. Is your Lucy four for four?"

"What are you saying?" he asked.

"That your lady love may be a gold digger. Her family seems to have nothing but are now marrying well."

"No, she's not." What would be his luck that she would be his secretary when he needed a wife?

"I hope not, Leo. I might come to the wedding just to see this woman. Tell me one thing you love about her," Kelly pressed.

"I love how she smells." He didn't lie; he always liked her floral scent. From the moment he had met her, he had liked that about her.

"Maybe by the morning of the wedding, you will have a better answer than that, Leo," Kelly said and squeezed his shoulder on the way by him as she went to get their girls.

He had said what he thought she wanted to hear. What could he tell her? That he loved how she had looked at him when he had checked her body for injuries that morning? The way her breath caught when his hands had grazed her breasts? That she tasted like heaven and red sauce? That was not something he could tell his ex-wife, no matter how close they were.

CHAPTER SEVENTEEN

GOING over Leo's work week with him on Monday morning had Lucy asking him if he was taking the day off on Wednesday for their wedding. Never would she have thought that she would be asking that of her boss. Nor would she have thought she would be excited about it. *They were getting married this week!*

That morning when she had woken up without him beside her, she had realized she missed him. It had only been two days, for god's sake. No way was she attached to him that much.

"You have nothing in the calendar for tonight, and my mom has invited us out for supper," she said, not wanting to spend an evening with Sera, Harrison, and Leo. She didn't think she could prove to her mom one-on-one that they were in love.

"Sure. I would love to." He grinned, but she didn't feel his confidence.

"Sera's making the reservations, and I'll tell you where once she tells me. I think it will be nearby since we all work around here." She was rambling, trying not to look at her giant ring. That made Leo smile.

She had forgotten it when she went dress shopping with her sister, still not used to wearing it yet. By the time she remembered it, it was only her and Agatha at home, and Agatha didn't care about the ring.

"I look forward to meeting the woman who taught you how to start a food fight." He leaned back in his chair.

"I have all the clothes washed, and all the stains came out. Well, all except my shirt, but I knew that would be lost. I also washed the clothes I wore home, and I'll bring them back." She was rambling again, and at this point, she couldn't stop.

"You didn't have to leave so early," he said.

"I did. Mornings start early at the house. Breakfast starts around 6 a.m. Then we went dress shopping." She shrugged. He probably didn't care at all.

"Wedding dress? On a Sunday?" He leaned forward in his chair.

"Yes, Mom has a place. She's bought four wedding dresses from there within the last six months, so the owner opened just for her yesterday."

"Your mom has purchased four wedding dresses in six months?" Leo asked in disbelief, even if he knew that two of her sisters had recently gotten married.

"Yep. Agatha calls it 'the great Lovely fall' now. First, she fell for Harrison—Mom, that is. Then Maby and Cliff got together, still odd. After them, Harper and Kaine, and then Buzz seduced Jonas. Or he seduced her; I don't really want to know." She gave a little shake at the images.

"At least it worked out for us, and you could get a dress on a Sunday. Any pain from when your sister tackled you?" he asked.

"No, nothing. But I relaxed all afternoon and evening." She had rested all afternoon the day before, sleeping and watching TV like a teenager. Even Agatha joined her for a few hours, as long as they watched Bob's Burger's, which they did. Each stated that they were Louise and then spent four episodes pointing out reasons behind their decision. Lucy was sure that they were both right.

"Good. It doesn't take much sometimes," he stated.

"Did any of your wives miscarry?" She hadn't thought about it until he was overly concerned on Saturday.

"No, but Aubrey was touch-and-go for a while."

"I'm trying to be more careful. Mom talked to the girls, and I have until the wedding. She can't control them anymore after that." She grinned, hoping it would work.

"So, Wednesday?" he asked, shaking his head.

"It's a Lovely thing. We've started more bar fights between sisters than we have ever seen in the wild. And, oddly, we never fight over men," she said, trying not to laugh.

Leo grinned. "At least you have your standards."

"That we do." She got up from her chair. "I'll tell you when I know where we're eating tonight. Oh, and if you are interested, my friend Cliff wants to take you out for a drink."

"Cliff?" he asked in surprise. The name always made him think he was her husband. Even if she had said he wasn't, and he hadn't believed her.

"Yep. He's married to Maby, but he's also my friend. He says he wants to look you over." She sighed, whatever that meant.

"Will this be about kissing his wife?"

"No, she never told him about that. He just wants to meet you. He thinks I have a bad picker," she admitted. It was general knowledge in the family, so he would find out sooner or later.

"A bad picker?" he asked in confusion.

"I pick the worst man in the room, always have. You seem different, but we'll see," she said with a wink and left him to his work.

CHAPTER EIGHTEEN

Later that afternoon, his work was interrupted by voices in the outer office, or more precisely, a squeal of delight from the outer office. Getting up, he went to see what was happening.

Lucy was in the process of being hugged by her stepmom as the man who was not her husband looked on with a lopsided grin. Pushing out of her arms, Lucy said, "Settle down, Sera, it's just a ring."

"It's beautiful, Lucy Maud!" Sera gushed, grabbing her hand again for another look.

"It is," she admitted, looking at it as she wiggled her fingers slightly, either to make it glitter or because she was nervous. She hadn't said anything to him about it except that it was too big. But now she was admitting she liked it, or was it just a show for her mom?

"I saw it and thought of her," Leo said, which was true, but that was when he thought she was a cold, frigid woman. But the ring was still beautiful.

To his complete surprise, her mom's eyes turned to him, and she rushed him and gave him a huge hug also. It had been years since a practical stranger had hugged him for no real reason.

"It is *so* Lucy, Leo. You know her so well." He let her continue to hug him.

"I was hoping it was her." He hadn't cared much at the time, but that was before the food fight.

"Shall we head out?" Sera's husband stated from across the room. His eyes were on his wife, still in Leo's arms.

"Leo, this is Harrison and Sera Dean. Guys, this is Leo Montgomery." Lucy introduced them, though a little late since he had already hugged one of them. Not to mention he had met Sera the Saturday before.

Sera left him and put an arm around her husband. "I am so happy you stopped being mean to Lucy."

Leo looked at the mother and then the daughter, then back to the mother. "Me?"

"You were so mean to her those first few weeks, I almost had to come up here and talk to you. Nobody gets to be mean to my kids," said the woman who was barely older than her daughter.

"Sera!" Lucy stated.

"I just have to say it before we leave. I want you to apologize to Lucy," the woman stated.

Leo had no idea what to do. Never had he thought he was mean to her, but she must have said something to her mom months before, and it seemed the woman remembered it.

Turning to his fiancé, he decided to do what any good fiancé would do in the situation. Pulling her close to him, he saw her brown eyes go wide as her hard belly touched his stomach. Running his thumb over her cheekbone, he whispered, "I'm sorry I was ever mean to you, Lucy. Can you forgive me?"

For a second, he didn't think she was going to respond, but then she said in a breathy whisper, "Yes."

With a slight grin, he kissed her lips ever so lightly. He felt her take a quick breath just as his lips grazed hers. Today she didn't taste of red sauce, but of Lucy.

Stepping back for fear he would keep kissing her if he didn't, he put distance between them and turned to her mom. "I apologized."

"Thank you." Her mom was looking at them with moisture in her eyes.

"Here's your coat, Lucy," Harrison said, ignoring that his wife was crying.

"Thanks, Harrison." Lucy didn't grab her coat, just stood where he had left her. Then she gave a little shake and grabbed her jacket from her stepfather.

"I made reservations at The Merchant," Sera said to them, which reminded him that Lucy hadn't remembered to tell him that.

Grabbing Lucy's hand, they headed out. The walk to the restaurant was uneventful and silent for the group, which gave Leo time to think about the woman beside him. They had been engaged for three days now, and she was the same secretary she had been since the beginning. Nothing about the day said that anything had changed; only her ring was different.

This morning she was still perched on the chair when she went over his day, her fingers tapping the entire time. If she hadn't gone over their wedding information at that time, he wouldn't have known they were getting married at a small wedding venue just outside the city limits. Nor would he know it was happening at 2 p.m. and that his kids needed to be there an hour before.

He was thinking he maybe needed to have morning meetings with his new wife before they came to work. Preferably naked. Would she perch on the edge of the bed naked and tell him about his day? He was hoping she would.

Leo pushed those thoughts away as they entered the restaurant. His mind couldn't be on Lucy naked while getting to know her parents, or whatever they were. The group was immediately led to a table near the back of the restaurant. Once seated, he had to let go of her hand but found he really didn't want to. He instantly missed her small, warm hand in his.

Right away, the waiter came and handed out menus and took drink orders. No one ordered alcohol. Both women thanked the young man as he left the table with matching smiles and using his name.

"What are you having, Harrison?" Sera asked her husband.

"Steak," Harrison said without much looking through the menu.

"I'm going to have the pot roast. What about you, Lucy?" Sera turned to her stepdaughter.

"The special," Lucy said, not looking at the menu at all.

"Lucy always gets the special," Harrison said to Leo. It seemed odd that as her fiancé, he didn't know that, but sadly, he hadn't taken her out very much, and never as anything but an employee. But she had ordered the special then also.

"Not always, Harrison," Lucy argued with him.

"Harrison, leave Lucy alone. So, the wedding's in two days. Are you nervous, Leo?" Sera turned to him.

"Not at all. Maybe when the time is closer," Leo admitted. He had no second thoughts about marrying Lucy. It was still exactly what he wanted, and it was getting better all the time.

"Lucy, how about you?" Sera turned to her.

"I don't know, maybe. I've never been married before, so it is all new to me." She was spinning her ring on her finger.

"Isn't the first one always the practice one?" Harrison laughed at his own joke, but the women did not. They just glared at him. "Hey, except Lucy, we have all been married before."

"Not funny, Harrison Dean." Sera frowned.

"I'm betting Harrison's second marriage is about over." Lucy was unable to hide her smirk as she said it.

"This one is not over, Lucy Maud!" Sera was the one who took offense at her words.

Just then, the waiter came up to take their orders, but the women could only glare at each other. Without looking, Leo ordered the special as well. As the waiter walked away, Leo assumed the argument would continue.

He tried to defuse the fight. "So, what's the craziest thing Lucy has done?"

"Lucy?" Sera looked at him and laughed. "Lucy's done it all."

"Thank you, Mom," Lucy said sarcastically, taking a drink of her water.

"But you have, Lucy! The first time I met her, she had Buzz by the ankles and was dangling her from the railing at the house. Buzz was ten, and Lucy was fourteen, and they were, of course, fighting over something."

"That was Mabel. We just told you the wrong names that day. I was the one who was going to catch her if she fell." Lucy grinned. "Or not."

"Within a week, Lucy had been suspended from school for showing all the third-graders how to sneak onto the roof of the school and handing out cigarettes. And I was nineteen, dealing with that." Sera laughed.

"That did not happen! It was a few sixth-graders, and they were already smoking by then. I was just showing them a place to do it," Lucy defended herself with a smirk.

"You used to smoke in the house all the time like I wouldn't notice! It took years to get that smell out of your room. That's why Maby moved out of the room you shared."

"Ha! Maby smoked too. She moved out because I kept bringing Kyle Reed home after school," Lucy said, laughing. Then her face turned red as she stopped suddenly and looked at him. "To do homework."

Watching her finally relax, Leo leaned back in his chair and was surprised she was still nervously tapping her fingers on the table, even when she was relaxed and talking to her mom.

"Homework. I *wish* you had done homework. All of you little heathens. Fourteen!" Sera ignored her daughter's embarrassment.

"Don't go all innocent on me, Seraphina! You were knocked up when you married Dad," Lucy said with a smirk at Harrison.

Sera folded her arms. "I was *not* fourteen."

"Nor was I," Lucy said and laughed at her mother's mouth dropping.

"At least it didn't happen on my watch." Sera rubbed her eyes, probably seeing the preteen Lucy had once been.

"You can't talk. you brought home your share of gentlemen after dad left." Lucy pointed at her with her fork.

"Peanuts compared to the revolving door to your room." Sera laughed.

Lucy slammed her hands to her chest and pretended to pull something from there. Handing the invisible item to her mom, she laughed. "Direct hit, Mother. Probably because you were jealous." Her mom threw the invisible item at her daughter.

"From what I hear, it was a carousel of men for a few years at the Lovely house," Harrison told Leo, earning him a slap on the arm from his wife.

"Lies, all lies," Sera stated, but she couldn't stop laughing as she said it.

"What I want to know is why the men always had to go to your house." Harrison grabbed his wife's hands so that she couldn't hit him again.

"Because if you sleep elsewhere for more than five days in a row, you lose your room. That's how Buzz ended up on the couch the last year we all lived together. She had moved out for a week," Lucy explained.

"We were one bedroom short. When Harper was in France and Buzzy moved out, I split up the little girls into their own rooms," Sera added.

"So, Saturday morning, that's how it always is? All the time?" Leo remembered just how much the sisters fought, including the physical battle between Lucy and Harper. But mostly, it was just teasing.

"No, now that they're mostly married, it's quite relaxed—way less fighting. I mean, it's been months since anyone got a black eye," Sera said and pointed to Lucy.

"It was Harper, and Agatha gave it to her. Pointy little fingers on that one." Lucy laughed at whatever was going through her head.

"I don't think my girls have ever fought like that," Leo said, thinking about his own kids.

"Then you're lucky. I think I contributed to the situation, but you try and control the craziness. And it's not like Bradford had tried to control you five, ever," Sera said as the meal came, stopping the conversation about Lucy's crazy youth in a house full of women.

Both he and Lucy had gotten the fish, but she didn't seem impressed with what was brought to her. She just poked it with her fork as everyone focused on their own plate.

"You don't like it?" he asked her in a whisper.

"Just not what I thought it was going to be. It's fine," she replied and actually started to cut into it to take a bite, giving him a fake smile as she chewed.

"You can send it back if you want."

"No, it's fine." She took another bite, trying to prove it.

Harrison noticed they were having issues. "Lucy, is the fish bad?"

"Lucy doesn't like fish." Sera looked up from her plate and over at her daughter's.

"It's fine. I'm fine with it. I can eat the fish," she argued at everyone.

"Okay," Sera stated and looked at her daughter as she took another bite.

As everyone went back to eating, Leo watched her eat from the corner of his eye. She did hate it; he could tell she was just trying to get through it as fast as she could, but she wasn't willing to admit that she had ordered the wrong thing.

They ate, and he talked to Harrison as Sera talked quietly to Lucy. He tried to keep up with his conversation while but still listening to hers, but he couldn't. All he noticed was her laughing at her mom's pointed jokes and that she was sending them back just as fast.

By the time the plates were picked up, Lucy hadn't eaten but a few bites of the fish, but he didn't comment on it. She was an adult.

"Lucy, are you helping Harper this next weekend?" Harrison asked.

Lucy looked at him. "No, she hasn't asked."

"Sera is. I thought she asked everyone." He didn't notice the pointed look from his wife to shut his mouth.

"Not me, but I don't expect her to. She doesn't want me there." She shrugged, her eyes scanning the room around them, not looking at anyone at the table anymore.

"Maybe because of the wedding. Are you going on a honeymoon?" Sera threw in, changing the conversation.

Leo realized that there was something more between Harper and Lucy than the body slam over the weekend. He made a point to ask her about it later, but until then, he would keep a closer eye on her sister when they were together.

"I don't know," Lucy stated.

"Yes, but it's a surprise," Leo said, though he hadn't thought of it until Sera asked. That was how much of a surprise it was.

"That sounds fun. Just remember that Lucy doesn't like to fly," Sera commented.

"I'm okay with flying, just no window seats." Lucy was tapping her fingers like she was playing the piano one-handed.

"Any more Lucy secrets?" Leo asked since Sera was willing to share everything.

At his question, Sera looked long at her daughter, and he wondered if they were silently communicating something. What were they hiding?

"I have a few Lovely secrets that might help you," Harrison said, once again missing the communication. "They drive Jeeps and love eighties pop and country. They are terrible singers but love karaoke."

"We should do karaoke tomorrow!" Sera exclaimed, slamming her hand on the table.

"I thought we weren't doing anything." Lucy groaned as they watched Sera take out her phone.

"Nope, you are the karaoke queen. We must!" Sera started typing.

"She is." Harrison nodded at Leo.

Again, he looked at his bride-to-be and wondered if he really knew anything about her before they got engaged.

CHAPTER NINETEEN

WITH PLANS TO meet up the next day after work, at least for the women, Leo escorted her out of the restaurant. Sera and Harrison were paying the bill and had parked in a different area than she had, so they stayed behind and let the engaged couple leave.

On the sidewalk, Leo surprised her by taking her hand as they walked the short distance to her car. Did that mean he wasn't going to call the whole thing off? Because she would; her mom had not held back on the stories, and the only thing she hadn't told him was that Lucy was stupid, though it would've fit right into the slutty, misbehaving kid vibe the woman was trying to sell him. Unfortunately, it had all been true.

"So, what do you call them? Your parents?" Leo asked.

"Sometimes, but mostly just Sera and Harrison. Sorry about them, by the way. Mom loves to tell stories."

"It was interesting. I realized how little I knew about you." Leo smiled.

"So, who can I pump for information about your misspent youth?" She knew less about him, and after tonight, she was way behind on knowledge.

"Probably Kelly, my first ex. She likes to say 'she knew me when.'"

His words made her wonder what he had been like in his youth. His tattoo said that he hadn't always been as button-down as he was now, even if she couldn't see him that way.

"She's nice. Always willing to keep me up to date on the kids' schedules for you. The other, not so much." Lucy hadn't liked that one from the beginning. Kelly had always been helpful, willing to forward emails and activity schedules with her. Stacy had kept those things close unless she wanted Leo there or money to pay for the activity.

"Stacy can be difficult. Has been since the beginning," Leo said with a sigh.

"Yes, she can. I'm just over there." She pointed at her blue Jeep and pulled her hand away from his. "See you tomorrow."

"I'll walk you over there, Lucy." He quickly grabbed her hand again. "Why Jeeps? Harrison said you all drive Jeeps."

"Mom and Agatha can fix them, and most minor things we all can do. So, we get Jeeps. Harper has a Land Rover now, but everyone else has Jeeps." She leaned against her door.

"You can fix this?" he asked, tapping the car on one side of her.

"Some things, yes. Agatha is better at it, though. But if it doesn't start, you have to call Mom." She shrugged and smiled.

"Mom, who I just had dinner with?" He pointed in the direction they had come.

"That's her. She's willing to talk about my sex life and can fix a Jeep." Lucy blushed. Usually, she owned her past, but tonight it was awkward. Today it was with her fiancé, who she hadn't had sex with yet. "She can embarrass me pretty easily."

"I think you gave as good as you got." He chuckled and reached out to cup her cheek.

His touch shouldn't have been as comforting as it was, and she should've pulled away as fast as she could, but she didn't. Couldn't.

"Thanks. I held back, but so did she. There were many times where I had messed up that she didn't bring up."

"Because she doesn't always see them as mess-ups. That's what parenting is about." He leaned down and kissed her forehead. "Goodnight, Lucy. See you tomorrow."

He pulled back slightly, and she looked into his eyes in the dim light. Unable to stop herself, she leaned towards him let her lips brush his. Just for a moment, she let herself enjoy being there without being reminded that he wasn't in love with her, and he was never going to be. That it was all fake.

"Goodnight, Leo." She pulled away quickly, too quickly.

Frowning, he straightened and looked at her for a moment and said again, "Goodnight Lucy."

Then he turned and walked away from her, leaving her pressed against her cold Jeep, wondering how she could have kissed him, how she could have let it happen. She knew better. She was supposed to be smarter than that, except she was never smart.

Climbing into her Jeep, she was afraid that despite everything, she was falling for him. Stupidly falling for him.

CHAPTER TWENTY

It was odd that today was his last day of freedom before his third marriage. It had passed like any other day. Even meeting Cliff Scott at a dive bar downtown didn't seem weird or like it was his last night as a single man.

Walking into the Grog, which was the same bar his kid had gotten drunk in not that long ago, he looked for Lucy's friend. It was then that he realized he had no idea what he looked like. That was until a hand shot up and waved at him as if they had known each other forever.

Walking over to the man with a gray shirt that said "Grand Cannon" on it, Leo and Cliff shook hands.

"So, you nabbed my Lucy!" Cliff said in way of greeting.

"I did." He wondered how close they really were. The guy was married to her twin, her very identical twin.

"Do you think you're man enough? Lovelys are crazy!" The man said it with a huge smile on his face.

"That's what I hear, but Lucy doesn't seem too bad." He sat down across from Cliff.

"She has you fooled, man. Lucy is the *worst*. She can drink me under the table and has done so dozens of times. But she's as sweet as honey. Not as cute as Maby, but still cute." He grinned. Did he realize he said they were both cute?

Dismissing the statement, he asked, "How do you tell them apart? Any secrets?"

"I just can. After you meet them both, you know who is who. Their personalities are opposite. Well, they used to be, but they're a lot closer since Luce started working for you."

"So, no help?"

"I guess the one that stands out the most is Lucy has a hyperactivity disorder, so she's constantly moving. She can't stop it. Maby doesn't do that, but she can mimic it, so watch out." Cliff shrugged.

"I thought she was nervous and that's why she moved a lot."

If it was an uncontrollable thing, then he wondered if she was ever really nervous. Then he realized there were times when she stopped moving—was she nervous then? He would have to keep his eye on her and see if it was true.

"Nope, she's done it all her life according to Maby, but she doesn't have attention issues, very much that is. When she would visit my place, I would leave out little things she could monkey with when she needed to. The tapping gets to me sometimes," Cliff admitted and waved over a waitress.

"I'll have to try that, find some stuff. So, did you date Lucy before settling for Mabel?" he asked after giving the woman his order.

"I did not settle for Maby; she is the love of my life. No, I never dated Lucy or anything else. Lucy's just my best friend," Cliff said and waved at the door. "Jonas and Harrison are here."

Leo looked at the door and watched two men come their way. Each grabbed an empty chair and sat down, waving at the waitress to come back to the table.

"Hello, Leo, nice to see you again." Harrison shook his hand.

Jonas did the same. "I am married to Bea. Just married."

"Are you sure they're coming here for karaoke?" Harrison looked around the bar. It was quiet and a dive.

"Yes, they always come to the Grog, it's their home bar. I've crawled to their house from here myself. They hate to love this place," Cliff said, looking around as well.

The waitress dropped off Leo's beer and took drink orders from the other men. "I don't know if Kaine or Harper are coming. I have never seen a Lovely carry out a silent grudge this long," Cliff stated.

"I barely notice it. Sera said Leo here gave Harper a talking down about slamming Lucy into the wall." Harrison slapped him on the back.

"Someone's going to get hurt if they keep it up," Leo defended his actions.

"They do. Agatha had her arm broken, and they've all had so many black eyes and bruises on them. The sad thing is that they all do it, even Sera's gone after them," Jonas said with a laugh.

"No, she does not," Harrison argued.

"Oh, yeah. Buzz has told me some great stories," Jonas replied, and Cliff nodded in agreement.

Harrison just glared at him for a while, but Jonas turned to Leo and said, "When I first met his kid, the eight-year-old, she told me that every one of them had sex in the kitchen."

"At the same time?" Leo asked, remembering them all in that kitchen.

"No, at different times, but they all admitted to it one morning," Jonas said, chuckling.

"It's those morning meetings where everything usually happens. I wish I could go," Harrison said, and they all agreed. It seemed being invited wasn't going to happen again for Leo.

"Sorry, guys, Harper barely came." A blond pulled up a chair next to the table. "Kaine Hawthorn, married to Harper."

"Leo Montgomery."

"Montgomery?" Kaine asked.

"Yes." Leo looked at him, wondering if they had meet before.

"So, she's going to be Lucy Maud Montgomery Montgomery?" Kaine asked, grinning.

"I think she should be Lucy Maud Montgomery Lovely Mont-gomery," Cliff replied with a laugh.

"I don't know if she's decided what her name is going to be," Leo said. They hadn't discussed it since she agreed to marry him.

"Is she going to stay working for you?" Kaine took a sip of his beer that hid his smirk.

"Yes, she is. Until she can't anymore."

"Can't anymore?" Cliff picked up on the comment. "Is she getting a different job? Or are we talking little Lucys running around?"

"That's up to her," Leo mumbled. He'd have to hold his cards closer; these guys were listening.

"You had better get to work, Cliff. Maby will be pissed if Lucy has a kid before her." Jonas laughed at the happy guy despite being put on the spot.

"Nope, she will be pissed if I knock her up before she gets her doctorate. Kaine is the one who should be feeling the pressure. Harper is the oldest," Cliff shot at his brother-in-law.

"No pressure, gentlemen. I'm just enjoying my gorgeous wife for a while before I share her with our children. And her business has her swamped right now." Kaine grinned.

"I'm still enjoying my gorgeous wife and loving that she's carrying my kid," Jonas stated.

"You mean your spawn? As she lovingly calls it." Harrison pointed out.

"She has a way with words, that one." Cliff laughed.

"Need I remind everyone she was a reporter," Jonas stated, which caused more than half of the men at the table to groan.

As they chatted about Bea being a reporter, he looked at the men who just yesterday, he thought had married gold-diggers. If they had, they were all enjoying the experience. More than enjoying it actually, based on their grins.

"Buzz!" Cliff yelled from his spot next to Leo, focusing Leo's attention on the door.

The redhead in question just gave him the middle finger, two in fact. Sera and Harper came in behind her. Each were pissed, then happy to see their spouses at the bar, waiting for them. It seemed the men being there was a surprise.

"You are a jerk, Cliff," Bea said as she approached the table, only to sit on her husband's lap.

"*Me?*" Cliff played the innocent.

"You weren't supposed to wear the shirt! Mom said so." Bea pointed to his chest.

"Mom has no control over me. And my wife dressed me today," he argued. "And you are definitely wearing a shirt under that jacket."

"No, I'm not," Bea said, but she couldn't hold back her smile.

"You are such a bad liar." Cliff leaned back and watched the door.

Leo glanced over that way as well. None of these Lovely sisters interested him, even if they were talking with the bartender like they knew him well. Which they probably did if this was their favorite bar.

Harper walked over, carrying a wine cooler and gave him an even cooler look. She hadn't forgotten what he had told her about fighting with Lucy, but he knew one day, she would feel guilty about what happened yesterday. Once she knew about the pregnancy.

"Really, Cliff, no shirts," Harper criticized the man as well.

Cliff grinned at her. "Take off that cute sweater, Blondie."

"You would like that, wouldn't you?" Harper hissed at him.

"Nope, I have seen your tits, woman." He shrugged. "And her tits." He pointed at Bea and Sera as one. "Mom's too. Wait one minute, I have seen all their tits. I did take home my favorite ones, so you all can be jealous."

"Ten bucks says you haven't seen Agatha's!" Harper didn't even care he just said he had seen hers.

Cliff laughed and reached in his pocket and pulled out a twenty-dollar bill. He tossed it to her. "I have never seen Agatha's. I will get that back when I do."

The group laughed, the snarky woman on the third floor was a bit different than all the others, but Lucy wasn't the only one with a past in the family. But none of them let other's opinions bother them.

"Nick is setting up karaoke for us. He loves Lucy! Has forever," Sera said, not caring that he was there. It seemed the filter was off.

"Cliff says that he's seen your boobs, Sera." Harrison pulled her onto his lap.

"I am sure he has. That fool almost lived at the house for a year. And a fucking billionaire! I should demand you pay rent. You owe me big time." She pointed at Cliff.

Cliff leaned toward her. "I owe you nothing, woman. You need thicker walls or a blow dryer that doesn't sound like a Boeing 747 at six a.m.! Fuck, that thing could wake the dead."

"Hey, Cliff, news flash! I had to get ready for work," Sera said as if it were still happening.

"I needed my beauty rest!" Cliff countered.

"You were hung over, both of you were. But at least Lucy would get up in the morning. You slinking out of her room and hogging the bathroom was super annoying!" Sera folded her arms.

From a man who had not that long ago said he and Lucy hadn't been together ever, it sure sounded like they slept together a lot. "Best friends" was sounding more like friends with benefits to Leo. It was starting to piss him off.

Somehow, he had thought it would just be a few drinks with Lucy's friend, but he was in for a night with her family. A wild night for a Tuesday.

The waitress came around with more drinks and got more orders. Oddly, their table still only had six chairs around it, but the wives were happy on their spouse's laps. As conversations flowed around the table in all directions, no subject was off-limits it seemed.

His eyes were on the door, waiting for Lucy. When she entered, he knew it was her. Not because of anything she said or did, but because he just knew.

Before the last of her sisters followed her into the bar, the wedding march started to play throughout the entire bar, making her turn to the bartender with a middle finger and a grin. Seeing the crowd at the table, she stopped and shook her head. Both Mabel and Agatha beat her to the group. Mabel settled on Cliff's lap while Agatha grabbed a chair after trying to push Bea off Jonas's lap with a laugh.

To his surprise, Lucy walked over to him and did what everyone was doing and sat down right on his lap, like he had been hoping. His arms went around her like they did it every day. In his mind, he hoped they one day would.

"Sorry about this," she whispered in his ear.

"I might be enjoying it," he admitted. His hand slid under her sweatshirt; it was white today with nothing written on it. His hands encountered a T-shirt, so he didn't get to touch her skin.

"Congratulations, you too," Harper said, even though he could tell she didn't mean it.

"Thanks, Harper," Lucy replied with her fake smile. Her fingers began tapping on his leg.

"Sorry I can't make anything for the wedding. I haven't ordered enough food."

"That's okay. I didn't expect you to do it for me." Lucy's fingers stilled, followed by her entire body. He pulled her closer, hoping she knew he was there for her.

"It's nothing personal," Harper stated.

"I know, it's me." Lucy remained still as Harper turned to say something sarcastic to Bea on the other side of her.

Harper turned away from them, and Lucy let out a pent-up breath and started tapping again. He was starting to see that she didn't notice she did it. But when she was actually on edge or nervous, she stopped completely. He just wished he knew what had happened between the sisters.

As the group settled in, Nick grabbed the microphone and announced to the room that they were doing karaoke tonight since Lucy was getting married. Oddly, there were cheers from others in the room.

Nick laughed at the small cheering section and said, "There have already been a few requests, but first, let me tell you that Lucy was not the best waitress we ever had in this place, though Agatha was definitely the worst."

Agatha cheered at her name, as did their table.

Nick pointed to Agatha and continued, "But she was always fun. When I started here, she wanted to be a bartender, so I gave her a chance. Fuck, she messed up nine out of ten drinks. Even her favorites. But she was a great waitress and was always willing to sing!"

The table cheered again. It seemed she was the queen after all.

"So, for the first song, I'm going to start with one of her favorites to get it out of the way. And so you all don't have to hear her sing it, I will." With that, he started singing Garth Brooks's "Friends in Low Places," and the table cheered again.

Leo looked around and knew not a single person was drunk, they were just this enthusiastic while sober. Even Lucy was a bit jumpier than usual. But as the song started, she leaned into his chest and whispered to herself, "I love this one."

As the song started, she started to hum to the music, then sing softly. Wrapping his arms tighter around her, he enjoyed the sounds she made as she sang softly to just herself. He wondered if she even knew she was doing it, because nobody looked at her or commented about it.

As the bartender ended the song, he got a round of claps from the entire place, though he wasn't very good. Once the song ended, he took control of the machine and started another song with no announcement of who was singing or what song.

As the opening notes started, all the women at their table perked up, and Sera, Maby, and Bea rushed to the stage. The song ended up being a Juice Newton number that had him laughing at the women, and he could feel Lucy laughing as she sang along.

The next song was by Dolly Parton and had Harper joining the group. As they sang about working nine to five, Kaine hauled his wife off the stage before the song was half over. Harper was completely willing to let him do it as she laughed and tried to continue to sing but failed.

"All My Ex's Live in Texas" came on, and the girls sang through that one, and Harper rejoined them from the back hallway before the end of the song. Kaine sat back at the table, but his eyes didn't leave his wife.

It was the next song that had Lucy off his lap and on the stage before the first word was sung. It seemed all it took was a little '80s

Reba McEntire to get her into it. Not that she hadn't sang every word of every song anyway, but it seemed a song about New England had to be sung from the stage.

"SHE HELD BACK PRETTY WELL," Cliff said from beside him.

"I was really thinking she didn't want to," Leo admitted.

"Now they have to get Agatha up there, but that'll be a little harder." He nodded at the black-haired woman in the leather jacket who was sneering at the stage.

It took exactly three songs and a genre change to get her up there. When Paula Abdul's "Straight Up" started up, she swore and pulled off her jacket, tossing it at Kaine as she walked by and jumped onto the stage.

All the sisters hugged on her as she started singing just as badly as the rest of them. Oddly, it was this song that had them all taking off their outer layer, all but Lucy that is. All were wearing a T-shirt like Cliff's.

None of the shirts' sayings were spelled right, and nobody said anything about it at the table. In fact, Kaine pointed to the one Bea was wearing and said it was his favorite. Then added with a smirk, *to rip off his woman that was*. Jonas groaned and the rest just laughed.

After that, the songs went back and forth from country to pop, but never leaving the '80s unless it slipped into the '90s, but nothing new. The women knew every song, every word. There was also a lot of dancing, mostly just made-up moves, but they all knew them.

After a dozen songs or so, women started slowly dropping out of the band, as the men called it. First was Sera, then Bea. Agatha tossed up her hands when another Garth Brooks song came on. She jumped off the stage, heading for the bar.

The twins and Harper were holding down the stage until the song "40-Hour Week" came on, then Maby left the threesome for something to drink. That left Harper and Lucy, which seemed to be okay since they'd done the song enough times to know what they were doing. But when Lucy accidentally bumped into Harper during her mimic of a coal miner, Harper turned and pushed her sister, causing Lucy to stumble backwards and trip over her own feet. She teetered on the edge of the stage and then fell off of it onto the floor three feet below.

For her part, Harper jumped off the stage to help her sister, who instantly pushed her away from her with one hand while the other was holding tight to her stomach.

Cursing, Leo pushed her family away from him as he rushed to her. Stopping right next to her, he pushed Harper and Maby away from her.

"Are you okay?" he asked, crouching down to keep her sisters from her. Maybe he was being overprotective, but her sisters seemed to be the most dangerous at the moment.

She looked up at him, and judging by her scrunched-up face, he knew she wasn't okay. Shoving everyone away again, he lifted her into his arms and demanded of her mom, "The nearest hospital?"

"St Mary's. I will take her," Sera said. All the laughter was gone from her face, replaced by worry.

"No, I'll take her," he stated and hurried out the door with her in his arms.

CHAPTER TWENTY-ONE

SITTING in a hospital bed had not been how she thought she would start the day of her wedding, but it was 12:23 a.m., and she was there for the night. The not-so-happy doctor had informed her she would be on bed rest for a week after her stunt.

At this point, the babies were staying where they were supposed to be, but she was on an IV and hooked up to a few monitors to make sure that continued.

One minute she had been singing and dancing, and the next she was falling off the stage. Hitting the ground had hurt, but it had scared her more than anything. The thought that she could lose the boys at any moment had her shaking and crying.

They had left everyone at the Grog, but she was pretty sure they were now all at the hospital and waiting. By now, they'd know she was on the maternity floor and why. Her secret was out.

Leo had gone to find her mom so that she could explain in person, though she didn't know how far she was going to go with the explanation. Was she going to lie or tell her she was marrying Leo to give her sons a father? Sons, she had seen them again, this time with Leo. Leo had held her hand and squeezed it when the nurse had called him dad.

The door opened, and Sera pushed into her room. Stopping as the door closed behind her, Sera said, "Lucy, you have a lot of explaining to do."

"You're supposed to have a Cuban accent, Mom," Lucy corrected her.

"Don't 'Mom' me! Leo told me nothing. But fuck, kid, you are on the maternity floor!" Sera came further into the room.

"I think I'm pregnant." She tried to keep a straight face.

"Think?" Sera threw up her arms. "No wonder Leo flipped out when Harper took you down on Saturday. He knew!"

"Yes, he knew. And I think Harper is in more trouble with him now."

"How is the baby?" Sera sat on the bed.

"Good, staying put. They have me on some meds to make sure." Lucy pointed at the stuff near her bed, stuff she would never understand.

"I don't think you'll be getting married tomorrow," Sera stated flatly.

"No, I'm on bed rest for a week. Then we'll see where we're at or if I need to stay for longer." Lucy explained what she had been told earlier by the doctor.

"Bed rest is going to kill you, honey." Stating the obvious on a sigh, Sera took Lucy's hand in both of hers, giving it a squeeze.

"I know. Leo said I have to be at his place, and Harper isn't allowed in the house. He had already warned her once," Lucy said, looking at the ring she still was wearing, her hand still nestled in Sera's.

"I'll talk to her and tell her you are not to be pushed ever. I'll send Agatha and Maby over during the day so that you're not alone. It won't be as bad as you think." Sera tried to reassure her that she wouldn't die of boredom during the week.

"Yes, I will." Lucy rolled her head on the pillow.

"You are so cute. I have to text everyone that you're alive and so is the baby. I made them all go home, even Cliff and Maby, but they wanted to stay. So, what do you want me to tell them about the baby?" Sera pulled out her phone.

Lucy looked at the ceiling. "I don't know."

"Can we name it yet? Louis? Linus? Leo Jr? Lucy Jr.? Lucinda? Lulu?" Sera giggled.

"All Leo's other kids have names that start with A's," Lucy said.

"I like L's better," Sera stated and tapped her stomach for the first time. Then tapped it again with a little more focus.

Pulling back her blankets, Sera looked at Lucy, then her stomach again. Then she rubbed it and her own at the same time. "You're further along than I am."

"I am," Lucy admitted, watching her assess the pregnancy.

"By a lot!" Sera stated loudly, eyes widening.

"I'm right around five months." She bit her lip and waited.

"So, he wasn't mean to you at all!" Sera demanded.

"He was a little mean in the beginning." Lucy tried not to grin. Sera still thought Leo was the dad.

"Don't want to hear about it!" Sera put her hands over her ears and hummed.

"Don't ask then." Lucy giggled.

Sera touched Lucy's stomach again. "Only five?"

Lucy looked at her mom, the only one she ever remembered having. Never had she judged her, and this was no different, even if Lucy was judging herself pretty harshly.

"I only seem big because there are two in there," Lucy admitted.

Sera's eyes snapped to hers. "*Twins?*"

"Identical, boys." She touched her own belly.

"Boys? We don't have boys!" Sera giggled.

"Most of us haven't had any babies before, so we don't really all have girls, either," Lucy argued.

"Haha, now we only have four months to get ready for these two. Luke and Maynard." Sera tapped her belly again and then pulled the covers over it.

"No way. And they will most likely come early, so less than four months," Lucy admitted.

"I'll tell your sisters that you won the 'hide your pregnancy' contest, so they all know not to compete. No more secret babies in this family." Sera typed into her phone as she spoke. "Do you want me to stay with you?"

"No, Leo's here." Lucy hoped that was true. She hadn't seen him a few minutes and wondered if he had taken the opportunity to leave … she would have.

"Okay. But call if you need anything." Sera hugged her tight.

"I will." Lucy hugged her back as Leo slipped into the room.

Sera let her go and hugged Leo. "And you, too. Call if anything happens. Maybe I should stay."

"No, you go," Lucy stated from her bed.

"Okay but call me in the morning." Sera looked at Leo as she said it.

"We will," Leo assured her with a gentle smile.

Sera was wiping tears away as she finally left. Leo turned to Lucy and softly asked, "How are you? She must not be too mad at you."

"She was great, although nothing I have ever done was this bad. She didn't even blink when I said I was five months along. But she got excited about the twins." Lucy smiled at the memory.

"Twins are pretty exciting, Lucy." Leo sat down where her mom had just been, and rested a hand on her leg.

"You would think so, but when you're single and alone, it's quite scary to hear the word twins. And let me tell you, I have heard that word every day of my life." She ran a hand over the two little buggers.

He captured her hand on her stomach and said, "I don't want you to be scared about it anymore. They are as much mine as yours now."

"Luke and Maynard?" She quirked an eyebrow in question.

"As long as we are not actually naming them that, yes." He laughed at her.

"Mom named them that," she admitted.

"I still say no. But no A names either." He surprised her.

"But yours girls have A names."

"Six is going to be too many A's. We are going to have six kids." He squeezed her hand over the two that weren't even there yet.

"If Aubrey tries, she could have a kid before Mom and Harrison have another one, making her great-grandchild younger than her baby." Lucy laughed. That would be hard to explain to the twins. And maybe, just maybe she would have to.

"You are so funny. Aubrey is not having kids anytime soon." He scowled at her for even mentioning his kid and getting pregnant. Grabbing the bag, he took out his gift shop finds. "I don't know what you read, but I got you a mystery, a romance, and a thriller."

Picking them up, she looked at the pictures and ignored the words that were jumbled on the top and bottom of the books. Setting them down, she told him the truth, "I am not really a reader for fun."

He took them and put them aside so they were not far from her, but she knew she wouldn't touch them again. They might as well be in another language, because they were not in a language she could read.

CHAPTER TWENTY-TWO

THE POSITIVE ABOUT Lucy still being in the hospital on their wedding day was that he had nothing scheduled for the day. The negative was that he had to call both his exes to tell them that the wedding was on hold and why.

Stacy just laughed and said he wasn't in love with the woman, that he had just gotten her knocked up. She also said she might not drop the girls off at his house at 11:00 a.m. but wasn't sure, which meant he had to have Aubrey or Alexis at the house to make sure the younger two weren't left alone.

Kelly, on the other hand, was concerned about Lucy and was genuinely happy for Leo to have another kid. He didn't correct her that there'd be more than one.

"You do know, though, that your kids will be twenty years apart." Kelly chuckled.

"I do. I was just thinking I was done with the baby thing, but I'm excited to try again," he admitted. Almost losing them had made him realize how excited he was for them to come, just not early.

"You like the baby stage, Leo. Or at least you did with Aubrey; you were there with her all the time. Alexis, not as much since you were working for your dad then," Kelly reminded him. "I suggest you cut back your hours and enjoy this one, Leo. Spend as much time with it as possible. You might not get another one."

"What are you saying, Kelly?"

"That you shouldn't keep having kids forever, and if you love this woman, you should enjoy what that love created," Kelly replied, going all philosophical to him.

He grinned. "Thanks, Kelly. You should stitch that into a pillow."

"Oh, I might, now that I have time before the wedding." She chuckled and hung up on him. He really wouldn't put it past her.

Back in Lucy's room, he found her watching some old reruns. He didn't know if she was watching it or just lost in her mind, because she didn't turn to him when he came in.

He hadn't left Lucy overnight, and though he'd slept little, she seemed well-rested. But she was up by 5:00 a.m. and hadn't slept again in the last six hours. At this point, they were three hours from their wedding, a wedding they would not be making it to. But right now, he wanted to be her husband more than anything. All night he was the father, not the husband. He didn't want that to happen again.

"Are they letting you go yet?" he asked her. She was bored. Her tapping was constant and with both hands this morning. Sometimes her toes would go as well.

"Once the doctor comes through again. They took out the meds but said I couldn't wander the hallways." She rolled her eyes at him.

He sat down next to her. "How are you doing?"

"The babies are fine," she answered, looking at the TV again.

"And Lucy? How is she?" he rephrased the question.

"She's slowly dying. She is no good like this," she admitted, shutting her eyes.

Her expression of pain made him laugh. "I have a present for the soon-to-be dearly departed."

Opening one eye, she looked at him closely. "What?"

Digging in his pocket, he pulled out the item he purchased in the gift shop between calls to his exes. He handed her the little metal item and said, "It's a fidget spinner. Thought you could use it."

Lucy opened both eyes and looked at the item. He had picked the blue one for her, in honor of the boys. She took it gently from his hands and asked, "Why?"

"Cliff said you enjoy them." He didn't want to say Cliff told him her secret.

"You didn't have to, Leo," she said, still just looking at it in her hand. Like she had never seen one before.

"How about we say I wanted to, that I saw it and thought of you going stir-crazy in this bed?" He lifted her chin and kissed her lips. When she didn't pull away, his fingers slid into her hair. He'd been wanting to kiss her this way since seeing her on stage with her sisters.

A voice came from the doorway behind him. "Hey, some old dude is making out with my sister."

Pulling his lips from hers, he looked at the visitor, the redhead. She was almost full-on laughing at them. From her arms dangled a suitcase full of Lucy's clothes, and she was wearing Lucy's sweatshirt that said "O hi."

"Take off my shirt, Buzz!"

Bea wrapped her arms around the shirt. "Finders keepers, Luce."

"You found it in my room!" Lucy accused.

"I can't remember where it was. I might have found a fun 'Yellin Stan' T-shirt also." Bea dropped the suitcase on the empty chair.

"Mine too." Lucy spun her new toy in her fingers. Already forgetting she wasn't going to admit to him that she didn't know what it was.

"It was Harper's! She has had that one for years," Bea said, pulling off the sweatshirt to reveal another interesting red one that said "Can-can" on it. "You can have your boring 'O hi' shirt. How are you doing?"

"Fine." Lucy looked at her sister in the shirt, still spinning her toy. This wasn't the first time she had held one either.

"You always have to one-up me, don't you, Lucy? Graduate first, have a baby first … Fuck, why not have two?!" Then she broke down and laughed and rushed to hug her big sister in the bed.

"It's been hard staying ahead of you, Buzz," Lucy whispered to her sister.

"Damn skippy. Now you're trapped in bed, so we're going to talk." Buzz pulled the other chair to the bed by Lucy's head while Leo remained sitting by her on the bed.

"About what?" Lucy laid back down and shut her eyes but sent the spinner going as she did it.

"Are you and Mom going to race to see who can have the most kids? You will have six, and she will have eight, so it's not a stretch for you to have two more. You seem to birth litters."

Lucy opened one eye. "Litters?"

"Two or three at a time is a litter." The redhead put her feet on the bed.

"It's just two, a pair." Lucy grinned at her sister.

"Pair, then, but once they are running free, it will be like a litter. I ordered just one." Bea tapped her sister with her toe.

"Jonas wanted two. I think he's disappointed," Lucy said.

"Jonas has never been disappointed in me." The redhead winked at him. "Meaning sexually."

Lucy covered her face with her hands. "Not listening. He's my favorite uncle!"

"Yes, you are, and if Kaine's wife wasn't a shrew, you would like him better. My favorite is Bex; she can always make me laugh." Bea wrinkled her nose at her sister.

"I like Bex also."

"How is Kaine an uncle?" Leo asked, because it didn't make sense to him.

"Kaine is Mom's brother. Twin brother," Lucy told him.

"He was already fucking Harper when they met back up. And I mean *fucking*," Bea stated with a hand motion that Leo had never seen before.

"And what's the difference between fucking and *fucking*?" he asked the redhead.

"I thought you were close to forty, man. I can't explain these things to people who should know," Bea answered with a straight face.

"I will explain it later." Lucy patted his hand. He was excited for that conversation to happen; maybe they could do it tonight.

"Thank god. I had to explain it to Jonas, then demonstrate," Bea said, again with a straight face, but Lucy broke down in giggles.

"I'm hoping for some demonstration myself." Leo smirked at his fiancée, whose face was beet-red now. "Who's Uncle Bex?"

"Do not call her that! She will hate you. You remember Bex Carter? We talked at lunch last week. She's married to Mom's younger sister. The family had been estranged for years, but recently gotten to know each other again," Lucy said, still a bit red in the face.

Leo remembered running into the woman and the strange conversation the two had. Now it made sense that they were somewhat related but still virtual strangers.

Before the sisters could get into another fun conversation, the doctor came in, and Bea said she was leaving. But the visit had taken Lucy's mind off other things and made her laugh, which was exactly what she'd needed. It seemed that no matter which sister it was, she got along and laughed. Except for maybe one.

Soon she was dressed in her clothes from the night before, and they were heading to his place. Carefully, he helped her to the couch in the living room and then he took her luggage up to their room because she was sleeping with him, marriage or not.

CHAPTER TWENTY-THREE

AFTER ONE FULL day of bed rest, she moved to the couch for the second day of rest. The bedroom got old fast and Lucy needed out. Once moved Lucy was feeling okay with her situation. Leo had been attentive all day, bringing her stuff she wanted and even carrying her to the bathroom once. After that, she insisted she go alone. It was too much.

After work, Sera brought over a pot roast dinner that Harper had made for them. Harper stayed away per Leo's instructions but made sure they knew she would send something over every day until Lucy was on her feet.

To her delight and amazement, Leo sat with her and watched movies from her teen years, the ones she and Mabel had on DVD and watched over and over again, so they knew every line. They were still as good and witty as she remembered.

She was sure Leo didn't see them the same way she did, but she did her best to explain why they were good. Maybe she talked too much, but she was trapped on the couch, while he could've left at any moment. But he stayed all day and pretended to be interested.

"Which movie did you like best today?" she asked from her spot leaning on a pillow. He was rubbing her feet and not enjoying the latest movie on teen angst.

"The second one, with the blonde girls and the guy," he answered, running a hand over her shin.

"That's what they all were, Leo. I love *Ten Things I Hate About You.* It's one of my favorites."

"It was good," was all he said.

"You don't even know which one that was!" She sat up quickly, too quickly, because Leo shot her a look.

"I do too. It was the one with the cute blonde," he argued, turning to her.

"All blondes are cute, Leo. It's a blonde thing."

"Then I love this one best since she's a brunette." He pointed at the screen.

"Ha, you didn't like any of them." She burrowed deeper into the couch, tucking her toes under his butt.

"I liked that you liked them, that they made you happy." He placed his hand on her upright knee.

"I bet you like a good action flick, with fighting and sex everywhere." She pouted at his taste in movies.

"Really? Do you know how much sex I watched today? Your movies are full of it!" he argued, making her laugh.

"Teen sex is different than action movie sex. More feelings, less action." She knew this wasn't really a conversation she wanted to have with her fiancé she hadn't had sex with, nor was she planning to.

"Did we even watch the same movies?" Leo asked.

"I saw nary a nipple today." She folded her arms.

"But enough hints that they were there to last a week. I learned more things to do with your clothes on than I remember from high school." Leo leaned back on the couch and winked at her.

"High school is way better in the movies," Lucy agreed, leaving the heavy petting comment alone.

"College too."

"I wouldn't know. Never went." She sat up and put her feet on the floor, getting tired of this conversation.

"You should have gone. You would have liked it," Leo said, looking at the screen again.

"I didn't have the grades." She got up and headed for the bath-room, bedroom, anywhere away from college talk.

Leo let her go. He was starting to clean up the dishes they had on the coffee table. Turning, she went upstairs, knowing he would be mad that she climbed them herself, but wanting to go to bed.

Without thinking, she went to his room, knowing her stuff would be there. And it was. After washing her face and brushing her teeth, she changed into an oversized T-shirt that she always wore to bed, guessing her mom had packed it for her. She climbed into the bed she would share with Leo for two years.

Pulling the covers to her chin, she wondered how she was going to not get attached to him. He had just spent ten hours on the couch with her, even though he hadn't liked her movie picks. He was sweet and funny, and she was having a hard time keeping her hands off him … or her heart safe from him.

Because even if they hadn't had sex, she was falling for him. Or maybe it was because she *hadn't* had sex with him that she was falling for him. Oddly, their relationship was the longest one she had ever been in. They had known each other for months, had kissed only a handful of times, and were getting married soon. Her usual relation-ship was kiss twice, have sex, then try and make sex into something more and not getting it right.

It took over half an hour for him to find her, but she hadn't fallen asleep yet, just lay there in the dark listening for him. Then she listened to him quietly get ready for bed himself, thinking she was asleep.

His smell overpowered her as he slid in the bed beside her until he took her in his arms. Then he was very close.

He kissed the back of her head and said softly, "Goodnight, Lucy."

She didn't answer, just enjoyed the warmth of his body on hers. The feel of his hands touching her, first her shoulder, then down her arm until it rested over her hand that was resting on her babies.

Then his hand traveled up her stomach and caressed the underside of her breast, stopping her breathing instantly. As she silently bit her lip, his hand moved higher and grazed her nipple, which reacted to his caress, as did her beating heart, which started to race.

Her hands were clasped at her stomach, but the rest of her body went straight onto the betrayal bandwagon, and her body nudged closer to his, too close because she could feel his rock-hard erection against her butt.

At the movement, his hand cupped her breast through the T-shirt, and his lips touched her shoulder. As her body further betrayed her by leaning into his caress, he whispered, "I want to try out some of my new over-the-clothes moves."

That made her chuckle. Maybe he had been paying attention to her movies, or at least the parts he wanted to pay attention to.

After a few minutes of caressing her breasts, he stopped just before she gave in to her body's need for more. His hand left her breast, and he pulled her to him.

Kissing her cheek, he said, "Goodnight, Lucy."

"Goodnight, Leo," she answered back, wondering if she had done something wrong to where he didn't want to continue touching her anymore. Had he grown bored with her so quickly?

Her tears fell silently into her pillow as she felt his breathing grow regular, and he fell asleep, slumber that eluded Lucy for hours as she wondered how she was going to last two years with him.

CHAPTER TWENTY-FOUR

STEPPING out of the bathroom after his shower the next morning, Leo expected to see Lucy still sleeping. When his alarm had gone off, he had reluctantly let her body go so that he could get ready for the day. At that time, she had only groaned a little bit and pulled the overs around her more tightly.

But now she was awake and looking intently at her phone. As he entered the room, her eyes went to him, and she dropped the phone.

"What do I have going on today?" he asked because she knew, and it would take her mind off not going into the office that morning.

Sitting up, she watched as he pulled on pants and a shirt while she listed off the meetings he had scheduled for the day. He didn't know how he was going to keep track of everything with her not in the office to remind him.

"What are you going to do today?" He sat down beside her.

"TV, maybe a nap. Maby is coming in the morning, and Agatha in the afternoon, so babysitting is covered." She sighed.

"They are worried about you and the babies. Do you want me to carry you downstairs?" He ran a finger over her cheek.

"No, I need to shower and change. Maby can carry me down," she said with a straight face. In less than a week, the Lucy he knew had changed completely. No longer was she reserved and nervous. No longer could he call her an ice queen. She was outgoing and funny, and most of their conversations were specked with jokes and teasing.

"I would like to see that since you are the exact same size."

"But I carry my weight in my thighs, and she carries hers in her head." She laughed at her joke; she must have told it before. When he didn't join in, she added, "Because she is smart, and I am not, Leo."

"You are just as smart as she is," he argued.

"She's a college professor, Leo. She got the brains."

"And you just told me everything on my calendar for the day, and you haven't looked at it in forty-eight hours." He tapped her nose.

"Not the same. Maby is getting her doctorate in children's literature."

"So, tell me. Who is Lucy Maud Montgomery?" He changed the subject, he had to show her she was smarter than her sister, not tell her.

"Really? Maby would flunk you. She wrote *Anne of Green Gables*."

"Then who was Mabel named after?"

"Mabel Lucie Attwell was an illustrator of children's books around the same time period, and near Beatrix Potter, for that matter. I always thought Mom named us, and Dad named Harper and Agatha."

"And they are named for?" Leo asked with interest.

"Harper Lee, *To Kill a Mockingbird*, and Agatha Christie. Dad was a literature professor and Mom was a children's literature professor," she said. He had never heard her say a peep about her real parents.

"Where are they, and were they invited to the wedding?"

"Mom is in Chicago now, and Dad is still somewhere in South America. Sera calls Dad, she always does for our weddings. Jonas might tell his father about the wedding, who is married to our mom, Judith. Neither have come to any of the other weddings, not even Jonas and Buzz's. So, I don't expect them to come to mine." She'd said a lot, and some he would have to question later.

"I'm sorry your parents aren't going to be there," he said, wishing everyone she wanted there was going to be present. Even if right now, he didn't know when they were actually going to get married.

"Sera makes up for it. She is the best mom we could have asked for." Lucy shrugged.

"She seems to be." He kissed her lips and got up. "I have to get to work. Call if you want something or need anything."

"I will." She gave him a half grin that made him want to crawl back into bed and say, "screw work." But he couldn't, per doctor's orders. Last night he had almost ignored that and had sex with her. Her body had been putty in his hands, but he had come to his senses and stopped touching her. Just like now, as he headed for the door, grabbing his suit jacket on the way out.

Being in the office was going to keep his mind off his fiancée and wanting her in bed at least for a few hours. Tonight, he would have to keep his hands to himself.

Backing out of the garage, he slammed on the breaks when he saw Lucy fully dressed and standing beside a Jeep, only to realize it was Mabel. She was wearing a navy sweatshirt that looked exactly like Lucy's but with no writing on it and blue jeans. Oddly, she even had navy blue tennis shoes on, just like Lucy had worn the night she had brought Aubrey home. It was as if dressing alike was so ingrained in them that they couldn't stop.

Getting out of the car, he called, "Morning, Mabel."

"Morning, Leo. I am on the first shift of the day, but your door is locked. I didn't pick it, but just know that I can."

"I bet you can," he replied while going to it and unlocking it.

"Mom taught us the survival skills we would need, and picking locks is one of them." She carried a box of plastic containers into the house.

"I'll remember that." He chuckled. "Lucy is awake, but she's going to take a shower and change before coming down."

"Bedroom upstairs?" Mabel looked up the steps.

"Yep."

She headed that way. "I have seen her naked before. Looks just like this." She waved her hands over her body. "Give or take a few tattoos."

Watching her walk up the stairs, he wondered which one had the tattoos, then realized he had something to look forward to that night.

Or not, because he was keeping his hands off of Lucy. But in a week, he would look for her tattoos. All night long.

He was still thinking about those tattoos three hours later when Kalvin called. He hadn't talked to his lawyer since the day the man had told him to get married, a crazy idea that had turned into Lucy being his fiancée. And soon, she would be his wife.

"Kalvin," he answered with a smile.

"Leo, you sound happy." Kalvin had been his lawyer too long for him not to know his moods.

"I am. My life is going pretty good lately. What can I help you with?"

"Well, actually, nothing. Just calling to tell you that Stacy has chosen to stay in the city and will not be moving away."

Leo laughed. His plan had worked even better than expected. He wasn't even married, and she was scared she was going to lose her petition, which he was sure was correct. His home was more stable than hers with Lucy in it. Stacy wasn't married or even dating anyone long-term.

"You don't sound surprised."

"I'm not. It seems my engagement has had the correct effect on her."

"Engagement?"

"Yep, I got engaged last week."

"You know I was kidding about that, right?" Kalvin demanded, concern in his voice.

"You weren't, but I found someone anyway," Leo stated.

"How did you find someone who would marry you to raise your kids and not care about your cheating? In a week?" Kalvin asked skeptically.

"It was easier than I ever thought, but I will not be cheating on her." He knew he wouldn't be able to cheat on Lucy. Lucy didn't deserve it, and he wasn't interested in anyone but her, even if they hadn't even had sex yet.

"Congratulations, I guess. I hope we don't have to spend too much on your next divorce." Kalvin laughed at his joke.

"I think this one is it, Kalvin. Your gravy train with me is coming to an end," Leo said, hoping that Stacy would stop pushing for more of everything, and his days in court would stop.

"I'll believe it when I see it. You fall into lust, Leo, not love. Call if you need anything." Kalvin hung up, and Leo wondered if his lawyer was right. Was he falling in lust and not falling in love? Because this felt different than anything he had ever felt before. It should've scared him, but instead, he was looking forward to the future with her. Her and their family together.

CHAPTER TWENTY-FIVE

Hearing yelling as he walked into his house when he knew none of his kids were there was an odd experience. Setting down his briefcase, he walked into the living room to find Agatha sitting on Lucy, who was on the floor yelling at her sister to get off, but Agatha was tickling her. Bea was on the floor also, holding her arms down so she couldn't defend herself.

Before he could get them to stop, Lucy walked out of the kitchen carrying a bowl of chips and said, "You guys better stop. Leo doesn't like fighting in the house."

But the sisters were not listening, so she tossed the contents of the bowl on them. The action stopped with the introduction of chips, and each grabbed a handful of as they separated and started eating.

"Maby is a shithead and deserves it, all of it," Agatha told Lucy.

"Truth!" Bea yelled. "She is acting more and more like Cliff."

That earned Bea a handful of chips down her shirt by Mabel. "You two are annoying."

"You're rubbing our noses in your smarts!" Agatha argued.

"Not my fault I'm the only one who's gone to college." Mabel threw a handful of chips at Agatha.

"Hey, I went to college. Four years of it," Bea stated.

"Beatrix Potter, you should have saved your money." Mabel looked down at her sister.

"I happen to have more money than you do, Mabel Lucie," Bea stated with a smirk.

"The Scotts have more money than Jonas does," Mabel said.

"You do not have *all* the Scott money, but I happen to have all of Jonas's money." Bea grinned.

"I am out of the 'whose fucking billionaire husband has more money' fight, but let me tell you about this guy I met last weekend." Agatha stretched her arms out so that her hands were two feet apart.

"Liar, Agatha!" Bea threw chips at her and laughed.

"Really, you two. You both would be married to the same guys even if they had nothing. I know this because neither one of you has gotten a new car since you got married, and you both still steal clothes from each other. Beatrix, I am living out of a fucking suitcase, and you stole that shirt from me today!" Lucy said from the couch.

"Jonas will buy me a new car, I just haven't found the right one," Bea said, taking off the T-shirt and throwing it at Lucy but missing, leaving her in a yellow bra.

For her part, Mabel pulled off the sweatshirt she had been wearing this morning and gave it to her little sister. "We might be the worst women to ever marry into money."

"How are you doing, Luce?" Bea pulled on the sweatshirt and flopped down next to her sister.

"Good. Bored," she admitted. "Thanks for fighting, it was fun to watch."

"Anytime. Next time we can take down Harper," Agatha said, getting off the floor finally.

"Hello, ladies?" Leo said, letting them know he was there. But he wondered if they had known and not cared.

"Finally!" Agatha said, "I can leave. Her supper is in the oven, and she likes to sleep with a little pink blanket. She might cry if she doesn't have it. And I put a little whiskey in her bottle, so she should sleep like a baby tonight."

Leo couldn't help but chuckle at the woman as she left the house. Her snarky attitude was great. It reminded him of Lucy.

"Hey, Leo," Bea said and pointed at Lucy. "The buns are still in the oven, so we did okay."

"That's what I like to see. Did you make her day fun?" Leo knew they had.

"Yes, we did. It was so fun here that I came back after class. It's a nice house, but we might have cleaned a little. Lucy is a pig," Mabel said, looking at the chips all over the floor now.

Leo smiled. "I hire people for that." Lucy didn't have to clean up after herself.

"I would suggest getting another." Mabel toed a few chips into a pile, then found one on her shirt and ate it.

"So, who is working tomorrow?" he asked the two remaining sisters.

"I'm here in the morning, then Agatha," Bea replied, brushing a few chip crumbs from her borrowed sweatshirt.

Leo nodded. "Thank you all for doing this. I feel better knowing she's not alone."

"You are so fucking lucky Mom isn't here. That would have gotten you a hug." Mabel chuckled.

"And she would have cried," Lucy added.

"And Harrison would have slapped you and told you not to make Mom cry." Bea grinned.

"Well, I have to go. I've got a loving husband to love on," Bea said breathily, making the twins groan at her.

"I am going too. Supper is in the oven and all. Lucy knows the rest." Mabel waved and followed the redhead out of the house.

The door closed, finally leaving him alone with Lucy. She was in leggings and a green T-shirt that said "LLLINOS" in purple letters. It was way too big for her, but she looked like she was comfortable for her day on the couch.

"Thank you for sending reminders today. I almost missed my three p.m. meeting." He went over to her and kissed her forehead.

She gave him a lopsided grin. "I was just sitting here doing nothing. You have a hard time remembering the ones later in the day."

"I am going to change and then get supper ready." He turned to leave the living room.

"Okay, I will be sitting here, holding the couch down." She flopped back onto it and pulled a blanket off the back and over her head.

"Do you want me to carry you elsewhere?" He smiled at her dramatics.

A muffled "no" was all she said. Leaving her on the couch, he hurried to their room and changed into jeans and a plain gray T-shirt. Looking around the room, he didn't know if Lucy cleaned or her sisters, but the room was spotless, and Lucy's suitcase was gone from the floor.

Back downstairs he found her in the kitchen, looking in the oven. Her ass pointed at him, so he could appreciate it.

"What are you doing up?" he demanded.

"Making sure everything was going alright in here," she stated, as if that was allowed on bed rest.

He pointed to a stool. "Sit down."

"I'm okay. I'm not used to sitting all day for two days in a row," she insisted but walked over to the stool.

"You had better get used to it, Lucy."

"I just can't fall off a stage again, I'm not planning that. They seem to not be in such a hurry to leave now, though." She patted her belly.

"Harper was the only one not here today. So, why is Harper so mad at you?" he asked.

"I don't know, really. We used to work together, but she said I should get a different job, and I did. She didn't want me anymore." She bit her lip, but he saw it quiver before she could hide it.

"Something must have happened. Maybe you don't remember." Except her memory was excellent.

"I remember." She looked at the counter and watched her fingers tap.

The subject was making her sad. It made her sister mad, but Lucy just got sad. Taking her tapping hands in his, he asked, "Your twin said something about a tattoo and you."

"I don't have any. She does." Her smile came back.

"I don't believe you," he teased.

"Hey, I am not the one with a sleeve, Mr. I wear a suit every day to hide mine." She laughed.

He looked at his tattoo. It was old and just a reminder of his misspent youth now. "It's nothing."

"It is not nothing. This scar from when Maby and I crashed our bikes together at twelve is nothing." She pointed to a jagged white line on her arm.

"I got it when I was eighteen, and my band got signed to a record contract." It wasn't something he even thought about anymore, but once, it had been a dream come true.

"What the fuck?! You were in a band? What did you play? Tambourine. I can see you just tapping away," she said as she pretended to play a tambourine, just like she had on stage during karaoke. It made him laugh; she made him laugh.

"Bass," he informed her. Definitely not tambourine.

"I would have played tambourine. Do you have a record with you on it?" she asked with interest.

"Yes, one, but I'm not letting you listen until we're married."

"Grunge band, huh? That's a turn-off." She wrinkled her nose.

He grinned. "Rock 'n' roll."

She snapped her fingers. "Shoot, I was hoping for a boy band. I could use me some used-up boy band member."

Leaning onto the counter, he asked, "What kind of band would you play your tambourine in?"

"'70s pop, for sure. Tambourines fit right in there. Can you play guitar?" she asked, more interested in him than herself.

"Bass is a guitar, so yes," he answered, wondering how she didn't know that. But then again, maybe not everyone knew that.

"I always wanted to learn guitar. I mean, I play air guitar with my magic fingers, but I never got to play the real thing." She pretended to play the guitar.

"No band in your school?"

"I couldn't be in band." Her smile faded. "There was a test you had to pass to get in, and I never passed it."

"But at least you have your air guitar skills." Talk of school always made her stop smiling.

"You can't take that away," she agreed. "Supper's ready."

Turning, he pulled it out of the oven. Tonight was prime rib and mashed potatoes with carrots in a sauce on the side. Setting it down, he couldn't believe her sisters had created this meal.

"Which one of those three can cook like this? But please tell them that don't have to cook for us. I can order in stuff." He slid a plate to her and handed her silverware.

"There are meals for the whole week in the fridge. Maby brought them this morning," she said, and he remembered the box her sister brought in with her.

He took his first bite. "Wow, will they all be this good?"

"Yep. Harper is a great chef. She can make anything." She spun her fork in the potatoes but didn't take a bite, just played.

He looked up at her in surprise. "Harper made these?"

"Yes, nobody else cooks." She didn't stop playing with her food.

"But you. You used to help her cook." He remembered her telling him that.

"That's true. She is a chef, though, and I'm just a cook." She finally took a bite of the potatoes.

"I can't wait to taste something you made. Is this Harper's way of asking for forgiveness?" he asked.

"I don't know. Maybe Mom just is making her do it." She set down her fork. It seemed that she wasn't so hungry after talking about her sister.

"I don't think so. She would be here if I hadn't told her she wasn't allowed to be here," he replied, hoping it was true. The rift hurt Lucy's feelings. "If she's going to keep feeding my family, you should tell her that Amelia is allergic to nuts and doesn't drink cow's milk."

"I will text her, but as far as I know, nothing she usually makes has nuts in it. She avoids them because of allergy issues," Lucy explained, showing him how much she knew about her sister's business.

He changed the subject. "So, tell me about '80s country music. Why do you like it so much?"

"Mom loves it, so we always had to listen to it. When she moved in, the main TV downstairs was broken. Someone threw someone else into it, and the TV lost. So, it was Mom's tape collection or the radio. Soon, Mom's tapes won out, and we scoured garage sales in the summer for more." She ate a few more bites.

"And Reba McEntire is the one who gets you on stage?" he teased.

She waved off the comment. "I was holding back. I didn't want you to see how crazy it gets."

"I'm starting to get used to it. The epic battle taking place when I got home was fun. I think it was because you weren't involved."

"I can hold my own with any one of them. Sometimes two at a time, unless one is Agatha. Don't take on her unless you know she's drunk." Lucy laughed.

"I'll remember that," he assured her.

"So why did you quit the band? Were you kicked out because of your bossiness?" She took another small bite of potatoes.

"No, it broke up because the drummer OD'd. I realized I couldn't do it anymore without Alex, so I quit. Without us, there wasn't much of the band left. I started working for my dad soon after that." He shrugged. There was more to it than that, but he didn't want to talk about it.

"I'm sorry, Leo. Losing someone is hard." Lucy took his hand in hers.

"It is, but it made me grow up. Okay, Lucy, how close are you and Cliff?" He needed to change the subject and couldn't get it out of his head that they were in the same room in the morning.

"He was my best friend, then Mabel stole him."

"So, your sister is married to your ex?"

Lucy shook her head. "No, we never slept together. Okay, we slept together, but never had sex."

"That is not possible," he argued.

Her eyebrow went up. "I have slept with you, and we haven't had sex. Though I don't even know if I kissed Cliff. If I did, they weren't real kisses."

"And you weren't jealous of Mabel?"

"No, I am happy for her! Though I wish I knew he was rich when we were friends—I could have used less check-splitting," she mumbled.

Leo suppressed a laugh, but was relieved that she didn't seem angry or jealous of her sister. "He seems happy with your clone."

"We don't even look alike." She grinned. "I've never seen him so happy. So happy to be settled down and with one woman. I was worried when they came back and started dating."

"Came back?"

"Oh, Maby pretended to be me and went on vacation with him. He found out and tried to teach her a lesson but ended up falling for her.

"That happened?! He said Maby could mimic you, but that well? Can you mimic her?"

"Not as well," was all she said. "Not for over a day, but I don't try much."

"Well, I hope you don't have to." He grinned at her.

"I'm going to watch TV. You can finish eating." She waved her hand over the plates, hers was missing just the potatoes.

"Okay." He let her go; he couldn't force her to eat. It seemed she didn't want to eat what her sister made. Harper had hurt her too much for that.

CHAPTER TWENTY-SIX

By Monday afternoon, Lucy had managed to kick every one of her sisters out, though Emma was coming over after school. Thanks to her newly minted driver's license, she was a free woman. Or another babysitter, in this case.

She wouldn't be there for another hour, so Lucy was alone, and today, she was listening to a book on babies and what to expect. What she was learning was that she really didn't want to know what to expect at all.

Laying on the couch with her legs hanging over the side, she watched her fidget spinner twirl on her finger as she listened to the amazingly gross stuff that was happening to her body. She was sure that she was learning stuff that would haunt her long after the babies were born.

As the spinner spun, she saw a face appear near it. Jumping in fear, she let the toy fly through the air as she pulled her headphones off her head, sitting up quickly.

"Lucy?" the woman asked her. She was still wearing her red winter jacket and blue jeans but seemed like she belonged there more than Lucy did.

"Yes, that's me." She stood up, tossing the headphone on the couch.

"No, you sit. You don't need to stand; the doctor says you have to sit," she insisted, then went to get the spinner from the floor where it had landed.

Lucy sat back down and asked, but felt stupid for it, "Who are you?"

"Sorry, we haven't met before. I'm Kelly, Aubrey and Lexie's mom." She handed her the spinner.

Lucy looked at the woman closer. She could see the older girls in her features, more Aubrey since Alexis looked more like her father, but the resemblance was still there.

"The girls aren't here," Lucy stated. *Of course not, they're in school,* she thought.

"I know, I'm picking up Lexie here after school. Lines got crossed, but I had time to come over, and I wanted to meet you," she said, looking at what must be a scary-looking Lucy. Her leggings were twisted, and her red T-shirt said "Pens," all a mess from a day of just sitting. And maybe a stain or two from lunch in front of the TV.

"Not much to see, I'm afraid." She waved her hands down her body.

"Nonsense. Now first, thank you for bringing Aubrey home that night. I like that you will go out of your way to make sure my kids are safe." Kelly sat down in the chair Maby had dubbed as hers over the last few days.

"Anyone would have done it. I was just happy to be out that night and recognized Aubrey from her picture on Leo's desk." She shrugged, dropping the spinner because Kelly was watching it.

"Leo is very taken with you. I'd like to see him happy," she said, surprising Lucy. It wasn't an ex-wife thing to say. In fact, the other one hadn't even said hi to her when she had picked up her girls the last time.

"I hope to make him happy." She had nothing else to say.

"Are you going back to work, when you can, that is?" she asked.

"I'm hoping to go back by the end of the week," she replied, not that she was really looking forward to it. Someone else was filling in the calendar, and she would have to have someone read it to her when she got back.

"How about the wedding?"

"I don't know. I think once the bed rest is over, we will talk about it. I mean, everything is ready, we just have to do it." Lucy hadn't really thought about it. Most of her thoughts were on not moving too much and finding things to do while sitting.

"Weddings aren't your thing?" Kelly chuckled at her.

"Just been to many lately. Three of my sisters and my mom have recently gotten married. It's a lot."

"I read that they married well," Kelly said, nodding.

"I guess, but they're still the same. Only Bea doesn't really work anymore, and nobody has a second job anymore. They've been able to keep me company most of the time."

"But not today?" Kelly looked around.

"My sister Emma is coming over after school. She just got her license." Lucy grinned.

"I didn't know you had siblings that young."

"Emma is sixteen, and Violet is eight. Mom's kids; she's having another one a few months after me."

"I love that Leo is having another baby—he's a baby guy. I know he doesn't seem like it. He took to Aubrey like I didn't even think he would. By the time she was six months, I was sure I was in love with him," Kelly admitted.

"But you weren't?"

"We're divorced. I didn't marry the Leo you are marrying. I married the one in the band, even if the band was gone by then. By the time I was pregnant with Lexie, I knew I had made a mistake. He did too." She leaned back in the couch.

"I'm sorry." Lucy didn't know what to say about it. She was marrying that same man soon.

"Don't be. I found Bruce, and he's the one for me. I'm glad Leo is the one for you."

"He is." Lucy let her feelings out, even if she was supposed to be keeping them in. For this woman, she wanted her to know that she was falling for Leo.

"I told him to spend more time with his new kid. I hope he does."

"I hope so too," she said, but she didn't think he would. They weren't his babies after all, no real reason for him to care.

"I also told him not to fuck around; you don't deserve that," Kelly stated bluntly.

"Thank you, I guess. I hope he doesn't cheat," she mumbled in reply, but knew he probably had already. It had been over a week since they got engaged, and she had been on bed rest almost the entire time. Even if he had been with her every evening, he was gone during the day.

"I can talk to him if you need me to, about anything. I mean, we are friends now, nothing else," Kelly said as the door opened in the entry, and they could hear voices.

Both women looked at each other and got up to see who it was. It was Emma and Alexis, chatting about a movie they both had watched.

"Hey, Lucy, are you okay today?" Emma asked, turning from her new friend.

"Yes, do you know Alexis?"

"We're in last period science together and figured out we were going to the same place. So, I gave her a ride." Emma shook her keys in the air.

"I didn't realize you two were related," Alexis said.

"All her life." Lucy pointed at her sister. Oddly, it was almost the exact length of time Sera had been in the family.

"Mom, can I stay here? Emma has a movie I want to see. We will do our homework," Alexis asked her mom.

"Up to Lucy. She's the one who needs watching." Kelly pointed to her.

"I'm fine with it. You two go have fun," Lucy said and watched them head up the stairs to Alexis's room, leaving her alone with Kelly again.

"I guess it was a wasted trip, but I got to meet you, so maybe not," Kelly said as she headed for the door.

"Nice to finally meet you also, Kelly." Not leaving the doorway of the living room Lucy watched as Leo's first ex-wife let herself out.

In the time that Lucy had worked in Leo's office she had realized that his relationship with his two ex-wives was completely different. With Kelly, they got along and were friends, but that was so different from his second marriage. She wondered how long it took them to get to that place? And if or when she and Leo divorced would they be friends also? After all they both knew how the marriage was going to end, and when.

Lucy pushed those depressing thoughts out of her head as she headed back to the couch. She turned on her book again and tried to focus on it instead of her future marriage. Now that Emma was busy, she had more time to get through it, more alone time. More time to learn about the gross things that would happen to her body.

CHAPTER TWENTY-SEVEN

LEO GOT HOME in time to meet Alexis and Lucy's sister, Emma, heading out the door. They were heading to Emma's house for a sleepover. Somehow, within a few hours of knowing each other, the two were inseparable. But Leo liked that his daughter was getting along with Lucy's sister since they were soon to be family.

Lucy, he was told, was napping in their room. He liked the sound of "their room." Once the two were on their way, he headed up to see her. It had only taken him a few days to get used to her being there, for her to be home when he got there, waiting.

In the morning, she still filled him in on what was happening with his day, which he liked because she usually did it from bed, her hair still mussed up from sleep. But even better was when he came home, and she told him about her day. Though very little happened, she usually had an in-depth story to tell him about her sister's antics or a play-by-play of an epic battle between two or more of them.

He found her curled up on their bed with her dark hair spread over her pillow. Her body was covered in the silver blanket that was usually at the foot of the bed. He knew she was sleeping because her body was completely still. He decided not to wake her because she needed the sleep, so he quickly took off his suit and changed into jeans, then headed down to the kitchen to see what her sister had left in the fridge.

Every day, whichever sister came, they were loaded down with food. More food than they could possibly eat, even if all four of his kids were here. And all weekend they had just that, and the fridge was still full. Harper may not have been able to come over to help her sister, but she was helping in the only way she could.

"I can do that," Lucy's voice came from the doorway as he dumped a container of stew into a pot on the stove.

Ignoring her, he walked up to her and kissed her forehead. "How was your nap?"

"Good." She shrugged and shuffled to the bar stools and sat down.

"Did Alexis and Emma spend any time with you?" He tried not to leer at her long bare legs under her shorts.

She shrugged. "Some, but today was my last full day on bed rest, so I was trying to do it alone. My sisters have to figure out what to do with their lives on their own. I can't entertain them forever."

Smiling at her answer he went back to the stove to check the pot. "Except, I think you can. You and your sisters are very close. Have you always been?"

"Yes, I don't remember ever having many friends growing up, but I had Maby. And Harper is only a year older and then Agatha is ..." She stopped, getting off the stool and looking into the fridge.

"Different?"

"No, not really. She likes to act different, but she isn't. She is sensitive, always has been. She hides it differently than the rest of us, though," Lucy mused, pulling another container from the fridge and opening it to reveal corn bread.

"How do you hide your sensitivity?"

"I am *not* sensitive," she argued. "The kids are all coming over tomorrow, right?"

Leo let her evade the question. Or maybe she was answering it, because she already knew the answer.

As they ate the stew, they talked about his kids, his exes, and his work. It was something that he had started to notice: she was amazing at steering the conversation to him, and always back to him. She said very little about herself unless he asked outright.

The first day they had spent on the couch, he had learned more about her than she had let him see since then. He knew there was a part of herself that she wasn't letting him see, a part she had closed off and wasn't letting him in, a part he desperately wanted to see again.

"What are you doing tonight?" he asked.

"Netflix and chill, the usual." She shrugged as she tried to gather up his empty bowl, hers was still half full. He wanted to corner one of her sisters to ask about her eating habits but hadn't yet.

Grabbing their bowls before she could, he put them by the sink, then grabbed a bag of chips. He figured she would eat them because he had gone through more bags since she'd moved in than he ever had.

"If we can put that off until later, I have a surprise for you."

"What is it?"

"A surprise, Lucy." He handed her the chips and took her hand.

All she did was shrug and let him lead her through the house to their bedroom, which to him felt empty when she wasn't in it.

Letting go of her hand, he pointed her to the bed and went into his closet. This morning when he had grabbed his suit, he had noticed his guitar in the back corner. Instantly, he had remembered her interest in learning it. Now he pulled it out and carried it to her.

Her eyes lit up for a second before she got her emotions under control. He wanted that second to last forever, to see that happiness all the time.

"I thought you could play the guitar." He tried to hand her the instrument.

"I don't know how." She put up her hands and bit her lip.

He smiled at her. "I know. I'm going to teach you."

Leo sat down and leaned against the headboard. Then he pulled her onto his lap between his legs. Once she was snuggled close, he grabbed the guitar and positioned it in front of her. It was easy since it was in front of him also. When he had thought up this plan, this was how he knew he had to teach her.

"I'm not very good at learning things," she whispered as he positioned her fingers.

"Yes, you are." He left her hands in position as he moved her hair away from his face, loving the soft texture of it.

Back to her fingers, he showed her how to do a few notes, and then let her pluck at the strings herself. Within a few minutes, she was asking questions and adding notes together. He had been right; she was a quick learner.

Soon enough, she was playing herself, and he was getting distracted because she was in his lap, wiggling and squirming as she played. Her questions were asked with her head tossed back and resting on his shoulder, then she would hunch over the guitar again in total concentration.

Before he did something he would regret, he shifted her away from him and got out of bed. No matter how good she was doing, she was still on bed rest, and he was not going to touch her if there was a danger to the babies. He wasn't just protective of Lucy, but her babies also.

As he left the room, he stopped and watched her for a moment. She was completely absorbed in what she was doing, and it was adorable how her dark hair fell over her face as she strummed the instrument. Her fingers were carefully placed, just like he had shown her.

Downstairs he cleaned the kitchen, washed the dishes, and then dried them. He reminded himself that just last week, she had been in the hospital because of a miscalculation that had landed her there. He was still mad at her sister for that, but he would be furious at himself if he was the cause of it.

Mind and body back as one, he went back upstairs to show her more if she wanted. All he wanted was to make her happy, and he might have found something that she truly enjoyed.

At the top of the stairs, he didn't hear the guitar as he walked back toward the bedroom. At the door he saw her still sitting on the bed, but the guitar was lying next to her. What he noticed was her hands on her stomach.

Rushing the last few steps, he sat down as his hands went to her stomach also. "Are they okay? Are you in pain? We need to get to the hospital."

Before he could move, she grabbed his hands and instantly stopped him. Looking up at him, she had tears in her eyes. "I felt them move. Or one of them, or both, I have no idea. They have never moved before."

"They must love their Mom's mad guitar skills," he said, relieved that there was nothing wrong with her.

Laughing despite the tears in her eyes, she let go of his hand, and her own hands went under her shirt. "I felt it again."

"Where?" he asked, though after four kids, he knew he wouldn't feel what she was feeling. But her excitement was contagious.

With one hand, she put his hand on her warm, hard stomach. Then she sat there looking at him, her brown eyes concentrating. Before he could stop himself, he leaned into her and kissed her lips, needing to taste her and that infectious smile just once more.

Her arms reached around his neck, and she kissed him back as his tongue slipped into her mouth, intoxicated by the taste of her. Whether he pushed her back on the bed, or she went and he followed, he didn't know. Once her back was flat on the bed, his hands started roaming her body, touching every part of her he had been dreaming of.

With a growl, he pulled his lips from hers, not that he wanted to. He wanted to keep doing that with her until the end of time ... except she couldn't.

After catching his breath, he watched her do the same, her eyes on his until she looked away from him, and her hands pushed him away from her. He let her do it, but only until he was sitting by her.

"I have to ..." Her voice was husky as she rolled away from him.

Grabbing her wrist, he pulled her back to him. His discomfort be damned; she was crying. She pulled once, then stopped but didn't turn back to him.

"Lucy, what's wrong?" he asked softly, not wanting to scare her.

"I am … I am okay with you sleeping with other women. I had no right to tell you that you couldn't but also not sleep with you myself. That was selfish of me. Please just don't …" Her voice broke on whatever she was going to say. "I don't want to know about it."

"I don't want to sleep with other women, I want to sleep with you. I do sleep with you, every night. And I plan to keep doing it until you don't want me to."

"Leo." Her voice cracked as she turned away from him.

"No, Lucy, I haven't thought about anyone else since you agreed to marry me, and actually, you were getting in the way of me dating for months before that."

"Oh, please. I set up your dates." She rolled her eyes.

"And why do you think there weren't that many repeats? Because I was lusting after my personal assistant." His words were quiet in the big room, but to him it felt like he was yelling. Yelling something he had never admitted, even to himself since he first saw her.

She gasped at his words. "Whom you don't want to sleep with."

"I sleep with you every night." He reminded her, though he didn't admit how hard it was to just sleep with a woman he had wanted for so long.

"I mean sex, and you know that. You don't want to have sex with me. How long are you going to keep that up?" Her voice was shaky.

"Until the doctors say you can have sex again, Lucy. You don't think that I want you?" He grabbed her hand and pressed it to his erection. "I want you all the time, but you're on bed rest. And I am *not* going to be the reason you're back in the hospital, worrying that we are going to lose the babies. I have more control than that."

He had let go of her hand, but she hadn't moved it away. Her eyes were watching her hand just barely caressing him through the fabric of his jeans. Taking a deep breath, he tried to control his reaction to the touch but failed.

Through clinched teeth, he said, "Not *that* much control."

She instantly became bold and slipped a hand up his length as her second hand joined the first, but this one unsnapped his jeans and slid the zipper down, opening his pants. Shyly, she asked, "This much control?"

He let out a low hiss but didn't respond otherwise. He let her do what she wanted, because it was making him feel so good. Better than good, because Lucy was touching him. Now his jeans were no longer the barrier, but his boxers. He quickly reminded her, "Lucy, we can't have sex."

Her innocent eyes looked up at him as her hand disappeared into his boxers. "The doctors said *I* couldn't have sex. They didn't say anything about you."

"Lucy," he hissed again as her small hand slid around him and squeezed him gently. "We can't."

"I will be very careful," she promised and swept her hair aside before lowering her lips to his tip.

Biting his lip, he couldn't say anything more as her hot mouth took him in. This was not what he had thought would happen, but he wasn't going to complain, not ever. Her hand went up his chest and pushed him into the mattress as her tongue brought his body to the brink, only to retreat until he was almost back in control. Then she would do it again. And again until he couldn't stop himself from coming and coming hard.

He had been unable to even warn her, but he was sure she was aware of what was happening. She didn't even seem fazed as she tucked his penis back in his underwear and zipped up his pants. When the button was done, she said, "Don't worry, I didn't exert myself." Then she winked at him.

"You didn't have to."

"I know, but I wanted to. One day maybe you can return the favor."

"The minute the doctor says I can, and I mean *the minute*. I will have my personal assistant clear my calendar." Grinning, he pulled her to him and she went willingly.

"She'll remember that." Lucy snuggled into his body.

CHAPTER TWENTY-EIGHT

IT WAS FINALLY WEDNESDAY, and Lucy decided it was time to celebrate. She was off of bed rest as of her early afternoon doctor's appointment, one she hadn't told Leo about. She had wanted to surprise him that night, and she had a favor to cash in. And she didn't want it to be some afternoon quickie.

So, Lucy had demanded that Agatha bring over some things that she needed to actually make her new family a meal, not wanting to rely on Harper for them to eat. Today, the four girls would all be there at the same time since she had moved in. *Moved in? Had she really done that?*

Since the two little ones were there, she was going to make something simple: hamburgers and homemade French fries. Emma and Violet always liked it when she made it for them, so it should go over well with these four.

Adding to that a milkshake that was always a favorite of all her sisters. Except because of Amelia's allergies she had Agatha grab some nondairy milk when she was getting her ingredients. The secret ingredient in them was instead of ice-cream she was going to use frozen bananas. It was something she had saw on TV a few years before and she knew she could make it all work together.

Mixing the ingredients, she listened to her latest audiobook through her headphones. The book was about having twins—yes, there was an entire book about it. Some of the stuff they said was just weird, but some made her think about her and Mabel and why they were similar and so different at the same time.

Tomorrow she was back to work. After a week off, she had no idea how she was going to get back into the rhythm of working with Leo and his office staff. Though she knew it would only take a few hours to get it figured out, she just felt the task was daunting. To her surprise, Agatha had told her she could send her pictures of documents, and she would read them to her, which would make getting his calendar back in her head easier.

Preparing the meal had taken her longer than she thought it would since she didn't know where everything was, and some stuff she wanted to use he didn't have. While improvising with other items, she made a mental list of what she would need to buy.

Amelia and Addison were the first to get home, followed soon by Aubrey, who had picked up Alexis on her way past the high school. Lucy had been surprised that Aubrey still lived at home and not on campus, but the two older girls seemed to be close, and they even tried to be close with the young two.

Within minutes of getting home, everyone had scattered and left Lucy in the kitchen to make supper. By the time Leo arrived home, she had the meal almost ready. "Do I have time to change?"

"Yes, but hurry and bring the kids back with you." She was finally getting used to the idea of all the kids.

"I will. I'm excited to eat something you made." He kissed her lips, but she didn't touch him because her hands were dirty.

"It's nothing fancy," she replied, hoping he wouldn't be disappointed.

He smiled on his way out of the kitchen. "It looks like you worked hard on it."

"It's something I make a lot for Emma and Violet. Nothing new," she said as she added two types of cheese to the top of each hamburger patty.

"I'll be right back."

Watching him go, she liked the feeling of them together as a family with the girls. It was what she couldn't have hoped for when she had said yes to his proposal. Not in a million years did she think she would be here, happy.

After many trips with the food, including three with just the milkshakes she had everything on the table. After much experimenting she was pleased with how the food turned out. She had to admit they were better than she had expected when she had started them. Pleased with herself and her cooking, she smiled at the food spread out on the table and hoped she wouldn't have to start another food fight with the kids. Because today, she was hoping there would be no complaining about what was being served.

Realizing she forgot one more thing she then went back to the kitchen for the beans she'd added to the meal to resemble something healthy. After all, she wasn't feeding her sisters, these were going to be her kids. Smiling, she saw that all the kids were present and no one was complaining about the food.

"This looks really good, Lucy," Leo said, dishing up a plate for Addison.

"I just hope everyone likes it." She sat down next to him. It seemed it was now her spot at the table. She liked being near him.

"Can I drink this, Daddy?" Amelia asked, glass in hand looking into the milkshake in wonder.

Before her dad could say no Lucy jumped in, smiling, "Yes, Amelia, I made it special for you. No milk in it."

"Just for me? Thank you, Lucy" The little girl was smiling as she started sipping from the straw.

She smiled at Amelia, realizing that this might be her first milkshake ever. Amelia had gone her entire life not enjoying something as ordinary as a milkshake because of her allergies. Lucy swore she would find ways around her allergy as much as possible so she didn't miss out on other ordinary things.

"Did you buy these?" Aubrey asked, looking at her milkshake way more skeptically than Amelia had.

Lucy turned to her. "No, I made them."

Suddenly, Aubrey dropped the glass causing it to crash to the table, as she shrieked, "Oh, no!"

Lucy followed her eyes to see Amelia grabbing at her throat, and Leo instantly raced around the table to her. Picking up the girl, he shouted, "Aubrey, get the meds!"

But Aubrey was already on her feet, as was Alexis, and both were out of the room before he'd finished the sentence. Lucy was completely lost as to what was even happening and frozen with fear at what she was seeing.

The little girl's face was swelling before her eyes, and it was the scariest thing Lucy had ever seen. Both teenagers came back into the room with something in their hands that Leo grabbed from them, then stabbed it into his youngest daughter's leg.

"What the hell was in the milkshake, Lucy?" Leo demanded of her, his eyes flashed angry at her.

"Nothing! I don't know!" She could normally list all the ingredients but couldn't with his anger focused on her.

"Nuts? Did you give my kid nuts? She only has this reaction to nuts." Aubrey went into the kitchen as he questioned Lucy.

"No, never. I made sure no milk and no nuts. In anything." She couldn't move from her spot at the table.

"Something has nuts in it." He looked at everything on the table, like there should be a pile of them somewhere.

"I didn't bring any. I swear," she defended herself, but her knees were getting weak.

Aubrey walked out of the room carrying a carton of milk, it was almost empty. Lucy had used almost three of them in the milkshakes.

Leo took one look at his oldest daughter and his eyes went right back to Lucy, "I told you that Amelia was allergic to nuts and you used almond milk to make milkshakes? Almonds are nuts, Lucy."

Lucy jumped up and grabbed the carton from Aubrey. She could see the A now, but the rest wasn't anything she could decipher under pressure. But she knew she was to blame for all of this. Her stupidity had caused the little girl harm. She could be dying because of Lucy.

"I'm taking her to the emergency room. Aubrey, come with me," Leo said calmly, not acknowledging Lucy at all.

"Dad, it wasn't Lucy's fault," Alexis said, but everyone in the room knew it was. There was no way it wasn't.

Leo just carried the girl from the room with Aubrey following behind.

"Is Amelia going to be okay?" Addison asked. She was the only one still in her chair.

"Yes, she will. Dad will make sure of it." Alexis went and gave the girl a hug.

Lucy was frozen with shock. She almost killed someone. If Lucy had been alone with her, she would have died. She didn't know about the medication and had been the one to give her the food that would kill her.

As the front door slammed shut, Alexis led Addison, who was now crying, out of the room, leaving Lucy alone with the evidence that she was unfit to parent anyone. Not Leo's kids, and not her own. She couldn't read a carton of milk.

Before she'd thrown out every speck of the meal, she had made a phone call. By the time she had her bags packed, Kelly walked into the house. No knocking for her this time either.

Lucy was waiting by the door for the older woman to come. Kelly slipped off her coat and asked, "What's going on?"

"I knew Leo would trust you to watch the kids. I didn't want to leave them alone," Lucy said, trying to keep it together for just a few minutes longer.

"What happened?" Kelly looked concerned.

"I accidentally used almond milk by mistake, and it almost killed Amelia. Leo won't want to see me when he gets back."

"If it was an accident, it was an accident," Kelly argued.

"He won't understand. Can you give him this?" Lucy slid the ring she had gotten used to wearing off her finger and handed it to her. "And tell him I won't be going back to work."

"Lucy, I think you have to talk to him," Kelly said, shaking her head.

"No, he hates me. I hate me." She wiped a tear and left. There was nothing left to say.

Now it was after midnight, and the house was completely quiet. In the seven hours since Leo had rushed out the door with Amelia, Lucy had heard nothing from him. Had Amelia gone home? Was she still in the hospital? Had Lucy killed her?

No text or calls of reassurance had been sent, but no knock on the door from the police had come either. Lucy had no idea if the police would come or not. They might as well take her away; her life was over anyway.

One thing was certain: she would never cook again. Never would she trust herself and her inability to read even labels anymore. For years she had known items by their shapes and smells, but not anymore. No way was she ever cooking for her family again. It was right for Harper to have not wanted her in the kitchen anymore, she should never have been there in the first place.

As of now, she had no job, no prospect of a job, and was so pregnant that she had no idea what she could do at a job. Maybe her mom could find her something again. Just no office job. She couldn't do that if Leo wasn't there, and her job with Leo was over.

Her life with Leo was over, but her love for him would last forever. But now it was hers and hers alone. At least she hadn't told him he was in her heart, not that it mattered since she was never in his. Maybe in his bed, but never his heart.

Leo, she thought with a groan. He hated her, and with good reason. At least they hadn't been married yet, so they could stop this train wreck before he was saddled with her forever. He would find someone else to marry to keep his kids from moving, someone who would be a better mother to the girls. She may not be able to love them more than Lucy, but at least she would be smart enough not to have to read books on raising them. Hell, Lucy hadn't even read book on raising the older girls, she had just done what she had learned from Sera over the years.

In the morning, she knew what she had to do: she would start the process of finding a family for the twins. Tonight had proven that there was no way Lucy should raise them. Lucy and her stupidity had almost killed a child; she needed the babies she loved as far away from her as possible when they were born.

A text came from Emma just after 8:00 a.m., saying that Amelia was getting out of the hospital that day. The news let Lucy breathe again. Amelia was going to be okay, but it didn't make anything in Lucy's life better. It wasn't safe for her to be around anyone.

CHAPTER TWENTY-NINE

LEO HAD SPENT the night in Amelia's hospital room, not daring to leave her side. He hated that she had a reaction on his time. It had been almost a year since the last time she'd had a reaction. This one had been one of the worse, other than her very first one, and only then because he had no idea what was happening.

Stacy had been pissed when he had called to tell her that Amelia was in the hospital, and she was more pissed that Lucy had made the meal that sent her there, as pissed as he was at his fiancée. How could she have forgotten about the allergy? She forgot nothing.

There had been an epic fight in the hallway with Stacy about Lucy. He wanted to be on Stacy's side and condemn Lucy for what she had done, but she was his fiancée, and she deserved a little loyalty.

Amelia had wanted her mom more than him by morning, so he had gone home. Aubrey had left hours before. His oldest daughter had been with him at the hospital, and he had only belatedly realized he should have brought Lucy with him, except he was still mad at her, he reminded himself as he opened his front door.

"How is she?" Kelly asked, coming in from the living room. Her clothes were rumpled as if she had spent the night on the couch.

"Kelly? What are you doing here?" Leo asked in surprise. He was expecting one of the girls or Lucy, not his ex-wife.

"Babysitting. Lucy left. She knew you trusted me and asked me to come over."

"Thank you for coming. I think it all scared her."

"More than scared her, Leo," Kelly said and held up a ring, Lucy's ring.

"What?" He grabbed it away from her.

"And she said she couldn't work for you either. She didn't mean to do it, Leo. It was an accident." Kelly folded her arms.

"She used almond milk, Kelly," Leo stated.

"So, you think she was trying to kill Amelia, an eight-year-old, with a milkshake? Were you really going to marry a person you thought was capable of that? Or was it an accident? Did she just use the wrong milk substitute in error? Is she human, Leo?" Kelly demanded.

Leo shook his head. "I don't know."

"Then I suggest you let her go, because if you don't know her enough to know that, then you shouldn't be with her. I saw her, Leo. She was still shaking when I got here. She thinks she killed a child, Leo. Does she even know she didn't?" Kelly yelled at him, something she rarely did. One of the reasons their marriage ended when it did was that Kelly did not like to fight.

"I don't have time for this, Kelly. I have to get back to the hospital," Leo lied. He didn't need to be back until he'd slept, but he also didn't need to be yelled at by this ex-wife. He had gotten enough of that with the last one.

"Leo, stop acting like the man I divorced and start acting like the man Lucy thinks you are."

Shaking his head at her words he reminded her, "We are the same person."

"I hope you are not, for her sake," Kelly said in a huff, slamming the door as she left the house. Just like she had when she had left him all those years ago, and just like then, he was left hating himself for how he treated those around him.

. . .

THE FOLLOWING Monday morning was as sunny as any other for Leo, except his fiancée was gone, his secretary was gone, and he had missed a day at work, so he was still behind. Not that it mattered since his mind wasn't on his company. He was too focused on his fiancée and personal assistant.

She hadn't contacted him since Wednesday night, and he hadn't contacted her. He knew she was back home with Agatha and was still torn up by what happened—Alexis had told him that morning. Alexis had heard it from her new friend, Emma, Lucy's sister.

Yes, Lucy had quit working for him, but she hadn't come to get her stuff, and he hadn't boxed it up to send to her yet. Nor had he even thought about hiring someone else. The desk had sat empty for almost two weeks now and could remain that way for a little longer.

He had spent her bed rest week trying to decipher what the calendar said, finding a small pattern in the jumbled words, then losing it before he looked again. He had missed a few meetings that week and even more after Amelia had gotten out of the hospital.

Today he had a 1:00 p.m. meeting somewhere and with someone, but he couldn't figure it out. As with other days, he just waited to be late, and the person usually gave him a call about it. It seemed to work for now but wouldn't work forever. He would have to hire someone if Lucy didn't come back.

Mostly he expected her to come back, to at least work for him. But he didn't want her to just work for him; he wanted her with him always. He had looked forward to the days they would come to work together and go home together, to be the one who took her home and talked about her day with.

He was so lost in imagining his lost life with Lucy, he didn't notice her mother walk into the room. "Leo, I am here to pick up Lucy's stuff."

He hadn't expected Lucy to send someone to actually get her stuff. He thought she'd come back for it so that maybe he could talk to her, to see what she said about that night.

"It's in there." He pointed at her desk, as if her mom had no idea where her things would be.

"Okay." She turned and went back out.

Getting up, he walked into the outer office to find out what she was taking. It didn't matter; Lucy had very little in way of personal stuff on her desk.

He leaned against the doorjamb. "How is she?"

"If you cared, you would call her." Sera slammed the drawer shut on the desk, then opened it again and grabbed a small plastic case of something and swore under her breath.

Though he understood the anger, he didn't see it coming from this woman. This woman let nothing faze her, from a sudden engagement to a daughter halfway done with a pregnancy, to her own kid in the hospital and her not knowing what was going on. But now her anger was palpable.

"She left, Sera. I would have talked to her when I got back, but she was gone." Even he knew he didn't think they would have talked then either.

"You accused her of trying to kill your child. Lucy! Lucy, who couldn't hurt a fly," Sera hissed.

"You weren't there, Sera. I told her about the allergy."

"Did you tell her how to treat it? Did you ever sit her down and say, 'when this happens, you need to do this, or that this will happen'? She has never encountered that before, and it scared her to death."

He looked away. "No, I didn't. I guess I should have."

"Yes, you should have." She turned back to the desk and grabbed a second plastic tube and put it in her suit jacket.

"If she really is quitting, tell her I will give her a good reference." Leo watched as Sera looked at the desk.

"I will never get her into another office again, Leo. Any confidence she has gained over the last six months is gone. I spent sixteen years trying to find Lucy and I had, I finally had. But now she's gone again." Sera looked at the ceiling.

"Tell her she was good, that she would excel anywhere." Leo wanted to hug the woman. She so needed a hug.

"Not anymore," was all she said. "That's all she wanted, her headphones."

Watching Sera head for the door, he asked, "Would it be possible to let me know when the babies are born? I would like to know."

Sera stopped and turned on him. "No, Leo, I will not. If you want to know, you had better talk to their mother. Or are you concerned she'll rope you into being a father to them? Because I can tell you right now, she won't. In fact, right now … right now she's planning on giving my grandkids away to fucking *strangers*, and there's nothing I can do about it."

Her anger was all-consuming. "She had never thought about giving them up. She was willing to marry me to keep them."

He instantly regretted telling Lucy's mother that they were marrying for something other than love. All Lucy had wanted was for her family to think they were getting married for love, and now he had said that wasn't the case.

But Sera didn't seem to notice as she tried to rein in her anger, anger he could tell she wasn't used to expressing.

"That, Leo, was the Lucy that thought that she could do anything. That was the Lucy who never let anything or anyone get her down. This Lucy thinks she will kill them, and nothing we tell her has changed that." She turned and walked away from him, carrying what little Lucy had left in the office and his life away with her.

Her words cut him as deep as he was sure his words had cut Lucy. But she had brought the carton of almond milk into the house, and she remembered everything.

Sera had been right; he hadn't told her anything about what happened when Amelia had a reaction, or how to treat it. That had been on him. Maybe if he had made a point of doing that, she wouldn't have used the almond milk. Maybe he was also to blame.

CHAPTER THIRTY

Agatha had been there for her all week. Agatha had brought her food and water, and Agatha had dragged the TV from her own room down to Lucy's. Agatha had sat and watched what she called shitty TV with Lucy, and it was Agatha that brought her news of the outside world.

She brought news that Sera had stopped by, though Lucy hadn't wanted to see her. News that Buzz was at the house, but Lucy had sent her away. News that Sera had brought home her good headphones, which she would no longer need for work. News that the world just kept turning without Lucy, because Lucy didn't matter.

Agatha was also ready to quit her job of taking care of Lucy after a week. Though Agatha was secretly a great caregiver, even she had her limits, and that line was Julia Roberts movies. How had the sisters lived together for so long and Lucy not know that Agatha had such a deep hatred for a hooker with a heart of gold?

But watching the dark-haired woman in the plain gray T-shirt give her the double bird as she walked out told Lucy everything about her sister. One, that she had her lines, and Lucy had crossed one. Two, that Agatha was sadly eating more than she was, and Agatha wasn't supposed to be supporting three lives. And three, that Agatha had stopped wearing the T-shirts with the misspelled words on them. Lucy hadn't seen one since she came home. And four, that her sister loved her and was doing everything she could to help Lucy.

Everything except watch *Pretty Woman* with her, but after her dramatic exit, Lucy really didn't want to, either. Shutting off the TV, she sat in the silence of her bedroom and wondered again what she was going to do with her life. For now, she was home until she had babies. But once they were gone, she had to live her life.

All her past jobs had involved food, but she was over food. She was not to be trusted around food anymore. Cleaning offices again was probably where she would end up forever. At least she had a place to live, because her new wages wouldn't bring in enough for housing.

She tapped on her stomach, then stopped and ran a hand over it. Since her fall off the stage almost two weeks before, she had done what the nurse had predicted: popped. No longer would she be able to hide the little guys. Maybe because everyone knew about them, they wanted everyone to see them. Or maybe because Lucy had done little but lay around and think about them, they were trying to get away from her. Just like everyone else.

"How did I not know you were pregnant, Luce?" Maby asked from the door.

It seemed doorman Agatha had quit along with movie-watching Agatha. Lucy wondered if food-handler Agatha was still around.

At her twin's voice, Lucy turned away from her and looked out the window. She didn't want to see anyone, least of all the more successful version of herself. It just reminded her how much she had failed.

"Really, Lucy? You're just going to ignore me?" Maby hadn't moved from the door.

Turning back to her sister, she put on her best fake smile. "No, sorry. What do you want?"

"You happy again." Mabel took a step into the room.

"I am fine." She used her old response, but she had no fake smile to pair with it.

"Yeah, I can tell." Maby's eyes took in the mess of her room, from tissues everywhere to dirty clothes covering the floor. "Sera says you're putting the babies up for adoption."

Pushing a small mountain of tissues onto the floor, Lucy asked, "Did she send you to talk me out of it?"

"Yes, she wouldn't be Sera if she didn't." Maby didn't meet her eyes, just started picking up the clothes. "Are you going to?"

Lucy just watched her sniff-test every shirt she picked up. Maby tossed a red one toward the closet, then grabbed another.

"No, because I know you well enough to know you can't give these babies away. You love them too much."

"I can't raise them, Maby, not alone. I have no money, no job, nothing." She pointed at the closet as her twin picked up an orange shirt, hoping she wouldn't smell it first, but Maby made the mistake and started to gag as she tossed it at the basket, then quickly grabbed another and wiped her hand on it.

"And we both know that that isn't the reason you are doing this." She tossed the shirt, no sniffing.

Lucy couldn't look at her sister, so she started picking at her blanket. "I'm not smart enough to raise them, Maby. We both know that. You have always been the smart one, and I have been, well, me."

At her admission, a gray shirt hit her in the head and fell to her lap, a direct hit. Because Mabel was perfect at everything, including throwing laundry. Looking up at her sister, their eyes finally met.

"And what is wrong with you, Lucy? What has *ever* been wrong with you? You were the one who found Cliff, and it took me a year to see what a great guy he was. You knew right away." Mabel stopped with the laundry and sat on the bed, a black T-shirt in hand.

"That doesn't count; I wasn't there." Lucy dismissed it. Finding Cliff had been dumb luck, and her sister falling for him had nothing to do with Lucy. They did that all on their own.

"Lucy, you were there every step of the way. I let myself fall for him because of how he treated you, protected you. How much he loved you. I fell for him *because* of you." Maby folded the shirt on her lap, then straightened it under her hands.

"We were friends." Lucy shrugged.

Maby's eyes never left the shirt and her efforts to remove the wrinkles. "You were the one who told me that I should get my degree in literature, even if Mom and Dad had the same degrees. That it didn't matter what they did, because I was going to do it better. That I needed to do what I wanted to do."

"And you did, but it was you, not me," Lucy said, because of her sister's love of reading was such a defining trait that her not teaching it would be a waste. Maby never questioning her decision again told Lucy that she had chosen right.

"What about when I was eighteen and started dating that guy, Hank Lawrence?" Maby picked an invisible piece of lint from the shirt.

Touching her sister's leg, she reminded her, "I told you to never date a guy named Hank."

Maby let out a little laugh. "No, you told me you didn't like him. And when you caught him hitting me, you attacked him with a tire iron. I never saw him again."

"Nobody hurts my sister." She squeezed her leg, wondering if Maby ever still thought about him, and hoped not.

Maby clasped Lucy's hand in hers, then turned and pulled her legs under her so that she was facing Lucy. "How about when we were fifteen and I took Sera's Jeep for a joyride and didn't take you with. You were pissed at me, but you still took the heat, and Sera grounded you for the entire summer."

Lucy smiled at that one. It was one of the many times they'd switched places so that Maby didn't get in trouble. "It only lasted a week, and she forgot. Forgave. Quit caring."

"No, she ungrounded you because you jumped in front of that dog that was going to attack baby Emma and got bitten in the process. You had to have stitches in your leg. You sacrificed yourself to save a two-year-old because that is *who you are*." Maby touched her leg, right where the small scar was. It was so small, even Lucy barely saw it, and Maby wouldn't be able to. But she remembered where it was.

"Anyone would have done that. She was a baby." Everyone in the family put Emma in front of themselves for years. It's what big sisters did.

"Lucy, you were the one who slept with me every night for months after Mom left, and Harper said we were too old to cry. You were there for me as long as I needed you. You let me cry." As she said it, she laid down next to Lucy, causing Lucy herself to slip further into the covers and snuggle up to her twin, just like when they were little. She remembered running to her own bed before Harper came to wake them. She would crawl into her own cold bed and lay there, watching Maby sleep from across the room, knowing even then that she would do anything to make her twin's life a little better.

"You were seven." Lucy wiped the tear from her sister's eye.

"So were you, Lucy." Maby pushed a loose hair from Lucy's eyes.

Wiping a tear from her own eye, she whispered, "None of that makes up for the fact that I'm stupid, Maby. Always have been, always will be."

"You are not stupid, Lucy." Maby pressed her fingers against Lucy's mouth.

Taking her fingers away, Lucy held her sister's hand between them. "Let's look at the evidence. You are going to be a doctor one day, and I flunked out of high school."

"How about this evidence? You are outgoing, caring, and wear all your emotions on your sleeve. I, on the other hand, am cold, aloof, and almost let the man I love walk away because I was afraid he would get tired of me." Maby pulled their hands to her mouth and kissed Lucy's fingers.

"That is not how I see you, Maby." Another tear escaped her eyes, pain for her sister. "Nobody sees you that way."

Squeezing their still-joined hands, Mabel went on, "It's how I see me, Lucy. Because I compare myself to you, just not in the same ways you do to me. It's easy to be considered smart, but a lot harder to let people into my life who might hurt me. So, I don't let them in. Lucy Maud, I don't see you as stupid, and nobody else does either. We all see what you have went through to be who you are. And all without our help, even if we would help if only you would ask."

"I don't like to depend on others," Lucy admitted.

"But we are not others; we are your sisters. We don't ever care if you fail or succeed because we will be there either way. Every day and for every moment, whether you want us there or not. Just like now. We are here every day, all day long. Just because we don't get to see you doesn't mean we are not here," Maby replied.

Lucy's eyes widened a bit. "Every day?"

"And all night, Lucy. Because we're worried about you. We're worried about our babies, and there isn't anywhere we would rather be." Maby dropped her hand and touched the babies that were sandwiched between them.

"They are not safe being near me," Lucy whispered and covered her sister's hands with hers.

"When I think about your babies, I can't even picture you as a danger to them, Lucy. All I think about is you dressing them alike in tiny shirts that have some quirky saying on them. I see them snuggled up against you as you watch cartoon after cartoon all day long. I see you telling them no, but letting them get away with everything. I see them with *you*, Lucy, not some stranger. Because nobody can love them like Lucy can." Maby rubbed her hand over the babies the entire time she talked.

"I can't, Maby."

"Just promise me you'll wait, that you won't make that decision until you see them. Until you hold them. Until the moment you know you can let them go. Because if I know anything about you, it's that your head and heart are not on the same page with this."

"I don't have a heart anymore," Lucy whispered.

"Your heart is still there, Lucy. Still as big as it has ever been. Leo will come to his senses soon." Maby pulled her hands up and held them between their two hearts.

"It was all fake, Maby. He needed a wife to keep his kids in town, and I needed security for the boys. Everything was fake," she admitted, because Maby already knew. There were no secrets, even untold ones.

"Not everything, Lucy Maud, because a heart doesn't break over something that isn't real."

Lucy closed her eyes. "I accidentally fell for him."

"And he did too."

"No, he …" Mabel covered her lips with their joined hands.

"I am your other half, Lucy. I know what love looks like, and Leo loves you. Has from the first moment I met him."

"When he kissed you?" Lucy smiled. It had been a long time since there had been a wrong twin kiss in the house.

"When he kissed me and looked at me in such disappointment and confusion. Disappointment that vanished when he saw you. Then he lit up and nearly ran to you."

"He didn't run."

"Maybe not, but he could tell us apart before he even knew I existed. And he was willing to fight for you without even knowing why. He'd protect you from everyone and everything. I knew he loved you then, and I loved him because of it."

"He doesn't love me anymore."

Maby, touched her cheek. "Months ago, when you were trying to knock some sense into me about Cliff, you said that Cliff was my Lucy. That I needed that touch of wild in my life. At the time I thought that you were full of it, but it's true. I love that he's always doing the unexpected and keeps me on my toes. He never lets me get boring and stale. I thought that you needed someone like me: boring and laid back. But in reality, you need someone like me, someone who loves unconditionally and has your back, no matter what. Leo does that."

"He will never forgive me."

"He will once you forgive yourself. Can you do that?"

"No," Lucy admitted the truth, there was no forgiving herself for hurting Amelia.

Mabel rested her forehead against Lucy's. "I forgive you, even if you can't. And I will be here as long as you need me to be here. Because you are my Lucy."

"Maby, I—"

"My Lucy," Maby said softly and stared into her eyes.

Looking into her twin's eyes, she wondered if Maby was right. Did Leo love her? Probably not back when Maby said he did, but by the end? When they were happy?

Lucy watched as Maby's blinks got longer and longer, until she stopped opening her eyes. Then she followed her sister into a dreamland where nobody thought she was capable of hurting anyone.

CHAPTER THIRTY-ONE

"Dad, are you busy?" Aubrey looked into Leo's office. Over the last three weeks, she had been acting as his personal assistant and was doing better than he had thought she would. But not as good as his last one. Not that he was comparing them or thinking about Lucy constantly.

"Sure, what do you want?" He smiled at her. Usually, she didn't care if he was busy or not before entering his office.

"I just got back from class, so I'm here the rest of the day," she stated, not something she usually announced. Since it was a school day, she was in jeans and a T-shirt, one that said "VVyomlny" in purple. He just chocked it up to teenage fads.

"Okay, thanks for telling me," he said, going back to the document he was writing.

"That wasn't what I wanted to talk to you about, what we wanted to talk to you about," Aubrey replied and looked behind her as Alexis came into the room, dressed about the same. Her shirt was gray and said, "Grand Cannon."

"Alexis, shouldn't you be in school?" He checked the time once again and saw it was just after noon.

"I um, we, wanted to talk to you," Alexis said, looking at her sister, who pushed her more into the room. It seemed his younger daughter was the one who needed to talk to him.

Turning away from his computer, he got up and led the girls to the couch in the corner of his office. Whatever this was about was serious.

"Okay, what did you want to talk about?"

The sisters looked at each other, and Aubrey started, "We think you need to talk to Lucy. You were happy with her, and we want you two back together."

"You were against me getting married again," he reminded them, though they had very much changed their minds before the engagement ended.

"We were never against you marrying her," Aubrey stated, as if she wasn't lying. "But you were happy with her, and she was fun to have around. Way better then Stacy. Since she left, you have been, shall we say, a bear?"

"Sorry your lives have been so bad." He folded his arms, the girls were barely with him, so they could hardly complain about his attitude.

Aubrey gave him a look. "Our lives have been fine, Dad. Yours hasn't."

"You two are wasting your time. What Lucy did was unforgivable. You two should know that since Amelia is your sister."

"She wants Lucy back too, Dad. She has forgiven her. Lucy just made a mistake," Aubrey argued, and she nudged her sister, who seemed to ignore her.

"Amelia doesn't know Lucy like I know her, girls. Lucy has an amazing memory that has never failed her. And she was the one who brought almond milk into the house. You both know that," Leo reminded them.

"Dad, it was Agatha who brought it in. She brought over all the ingredients that day," Alexis explained, leaning forward on the couch.

"So, it's all Agatha's fault?"

Aubrey looked at her sister and back at him. "Agatha didn't know Amelia had a nut allergy, just that she needed to buy nondairy milk, and she picked the wrong one. Only Harper knew, because she made all the food."

"Lucy used the milk, not Agatha. I will not blame her for this," Leo stated.

"Nobody is blaming Agatha; she didn't know. But you also shouldn't be blaming Lucy. She would never have used the milk if she had known what kind it was," Aubrey said and nudged her sister again.

He gave them a flat look. "It was written on the carton."

At his words, Aubrey leaned into her sister and whispered in her ear, which Alexis hissed back at her, "I promised I wouldn't tell."

"Tell him," Aubrey said louder.

"Just tell me, Lexie, or Aubrey will, I assume."

"I promised Emma I wouldn't. She told me in confidence, and I don't tell secrets," Alexis said, looking at her sister.

Aubrey rolled her eyes. "You told me."

"Because you were pinching me."

"I will do it again," Aubrey said and then turned to her dad. "Lucy can't read."

Alexis pushed her sister and stated before he could get anything out, "She has dyslexia. She can read, just not well. Lucy had no idea what was written on that bottle, Dad. She has no idea what is written on the papers on your desk. She has severe dyslexia and reads at a second grade level at best. Mostly, she doesn't even try anymore. She memorizes things so she doesn't have to read them."

"She proofread documents for me, Alexis."

"Probably just like I do, Dad. I don't. You're a perfectionist, and there is never an error. I just send them out," Aubrey admitted, not even caring that it was a part of her job to proofread the documents.

"No, she had them read to her by the computer. Sera took her headphones the day she came in. All computers have the option; it's in the settings. Phones too. The week she was on bed rest, she had books read to her. I saw her," Alexis explained.

"Emma told you this?" he asked her.

"Yeah, kind of. I spent some time at Lucy's house with her sisters. There were a lot of stories," Alexis admitted.

"How is she?" Leo perked up. He wanted to know everything about her.

"I don't know. She doesn't come out of her room and mostly doesn't let anyone in. I never asked to go in," Alexis admitted.

"Okay, say I believe you, which I really don't. She graduated from high school. How is that possible if she can't read?" He folded his arms over his chest.

Alexis and Aubrey exchanged looks again. "She never graduated from high school. She dropped out in the tenth grade because they were going to make her repeat it. She got her GED later, but Cliff said that in reality, Maby did. She took the test for Lucy so Lucy could have a GED for job applications. Lucy doesn't do tests."

Instantly, his mind went to her sadness about the test for band and admitting that she hadn't even took it because she wasn't good at tests. He leaned back in his chair. Lucy intently playing his guitar floated through his mind.

"These shirts are her work. She didn't want you to know," Aubrey jumped in and pointed to her and Alexis's shirts. "But everyone else does. A few years ago, she had a screen-printing business for a few months, but it failed. They kept all the mistake shirts, and everyone always wears them. There are a lot of them. Everyone always chalked it up to Lucy not spelling well, but she didn't have to spell; she had to copy. All her clients told her what to put on the shirts. Still, most got misspelled anyway because spelling wasn't Lucy's issue."

"Why didn't she ever tell me?" Leo asked the two. Lucy could read; she had read most of his documents while proofreading them. His mind rushed to her calendar, her entirely unreadable calendar.

"I guess it isn't something you want to tell your boss. And she's always been embarrassed by it. Her sisters didn't know about it until recently." He knew it was the reason Alexis didn't want to tell him about it. She didn't want Lucy to look bad to him.

"Or her boyfriend, Dad. I saw the type of guy she usually dated, and they wouldn't care one way or another if she could read or not.

She's always hidden her inability behind her personality. Being the life of the party and dumb, until you," Aubrey added.

"She isn't dumb, girls," he stated firmly.

"She also didn't try to hurt Amelia. She made a mistake," Alexis said. "A dumb mistake. Are you going to let one dumb mistake cost you the woman you love?"

"I don't …" He couldn't even finish, because he did love her. He had since she had nervously agreed to marry him for her kids. She had put herself behind him, his kids, and her kids by agreeing to be his wife. Her only request was that he pretend to love her. Not even for herself, but for her family. It was that woman he had fallen for.

Aubrey leaned forward and squeezed his knee. "She came out of her room today because she has an appointment with her doctor. Maybe you want to go to that."

"I don't think she wants me to be there," he admitted. He had said too much.

"You more than Harper. She's the one who's taking her this time," Alexis stated and cut a look at her sister.

That snapped him out of whatever he was thinking; she was in danger. Again. "Fuck! I can't let her be alone with that woman. Where?"

"St Mary's. The appointment is in an hour," Alexis called after him, but Leo was already out the door.

No way was he letting Harper have another chance at hurting Lucy.

There was no way Lucy could control her pent-up energy today. This was her second appointment after her disastrous first appointment. Would everyone still be pissed at her? Of course, if they looked at her chart they would. Falling off a stage does not make doctors and nurses happy.

"Just pace," Harper said from beside her. Her sister, it seemed, was already sick of her leg bouncing.

"No, it just gets people nervous," she whispered. Her first appointment had probably sent four women into labor with her constant pacing.

Harper rolled her eyes and let Lucy's legs bounce beside her. "Thanks for letting me come with you."

"You followed me here," Lucy stated, tapping her fingers on her black leggings, the only pants she could wear now.

"I was driving this way anyway. I thought you might want some company."

"You stalked me."

"Personal interest in your private life, it's different."

Rolling her eyes, she rested her arms on her now protruding stomach. In the month since she had left Leo, her pregnancy could not be denied anymore. So far, she had narrowed her list of potential parents down to three couples, none of which were perfect. And she hadn't talked to her sisters about it, because they didn't understand.

She had just been putting the decision off, not wanting to think of a time when she would lose them. They were a part of her now, so she ignored the fact that soon they would be gone.

"Mom wanted someone here with you this time."

"I can do it on my own. I did last time," Lucy argued. She was hoping everyone wasn't angry this time.

"I know, but you don't have to do it alone. We are there for you, Luce. No matter what." Harper gave her a side hug that made some of the tension in Lucy's body go away.

"I know." She didn't want to talk about it.

What she wanted to do and what she needed to do were two different things. The babies needed to be away from her for their safety, no matter how much she wanted them close. Lately she had started to worry more about Emma and Violet and the other new babies coming.

Last week she had decided that once the babies were gone, she would move far away from her sisters and anyone she loved. There was no telling how she could harm them. How she was going to do it financially, she didn't know, but she was going. She had to keep everyone she loved safe from her. She loved them too much not to.

"OMG!" Harper whispered under her breath, barely.

Looking around the room, she immediately zeroed in on who her sister was looking at. Her ex-boyfriend Kevin had just sauntered into the room with a very pregnant woman, a woman who Lucy definitely knew well.

"Lucy Lovely!" Pam Andrews rushed up to her and engulfed her in her arms, as if they were long-lost friends.

"Hey, Pam," Harper answered for her and pushed the woman away from Lucy, giving Lucy room to breathe. Deep breaths.

The last time she had seen Pam was when she was still dating Kevin, and they were caught making out in the Grog. Kevin swore up and down that nothing happened, that it was all in Lucy's head, but what happened in her head never created a baby.

"How far along are you?" Pam ignored Lucy's silence.

"Not very," Lucy mumbled, not wanting anyone who knew Kevin to know the actual date. "And you?"

"Eight months." She ran a hand over her exposed stomach. Her shirt was short enough that it didn't cover the bump anymore. Not even close.

"And who's the daddy?" Harper asked, because Harper would.

"Kev. Can you even believe it? We are so blessed."

"Blessed it is." Harper threw her arm around Lucy. "Lucy and her boss are having a baby also. Five months, is it? Or is it six?" Harper looked at her.

Lucy glared at her sister for telling Kevin anything. Not actually saying, she answered, "Yes."

"Thank god. For a second, I thought it was mine." Kevin wiped imaginary sweat off his forehead. "Three babies this year would be too many."

Pam whipped around and looked at him. "Three? What the fuck! You said this is your first kid." She ran her hands over her bump again.

"Maybe first this year," Lucy stated. "He has five other kids, Pam, and I wouldn't expect him to be there for you or the baby ever. No money either."

"No, no, he promised we will be together forever. We're a family now," Pam told Lucy in a condescending tone.

"He was dating me when he knocked you up," Lucy reminded her.

"You're one to talk, Lucy. You were screwing your boss when we were together. Not to mention going on vacation with Cliff." Kevin decided he needed to say something, which was a mistake.

"You mean when *you* went with Beth? Where was Pam those days?" Lucy asked.

"When were you on vacation with Beth? You know I can't stand Beth." Pam seethed, turning on him.

Kevin tried to talk himself out of it. "Babe, it was a cheap vacation, and tickets were already paid for when we started dating."

"So, you were dating Lucy, Beth, and that young chick that was at the bar with you last month? When did you even have time to date Pam?" Harper asked.

"Aubrey, her name was Aubrey," Lucy provided.

"Lucy was cheating on me too!" That seemed to be his only defense, which was not going over well with Pam based on her expression of disgust.

"She only slept with him because you had such a small dick. She needed to feel something." Harper pointed at Kevin's crotch.

"That is not true!" Kevin stated, then looked around the room at everyone looking at them and announced, "I have a very large dick."

"Prove it," Harper stated. "Pull it out. I will admit I am wrong if there is proof."

Kevin had unbuttoned his pants before Pam stopped him with a look. It seemed she didn't need everyone seeing her baby daddy naked. Lucy was sure that there would be a lot of women who still would because Kevin was not changing for her, or for anyone.

Before he could get the button done back up, Pam's name was called, and he silently followed her to the back door and vanished. He didn't even look back at her as he went.

Harper leaned over to her and whispered, "So glad those two are not his. Leo is so much better than him. What did you even see in him?"

Shrugging, she wished she knew. Low self-esteem and willing to put up with a lot of garbage? Now she saw the error in her ways.

Despite her words, Lucy was aware that Harper knew exactly who the babies' daddy was. She had probably always known and was happy to go along with the lie. She still was, for that matter, and would forever.

Finally unable to control herself, she got up and started pacing around the room. It didn't stop the nervousness, but it gave her something to do. Most moms-to-be were on their phones, something Lucy couldn't do much of. For a moment she wished the waiting room had a window, something for her to look at.

Back and forth she paced, and Harper soon gave up her chair to a woman who had just arrived. Her sister leaned against the wall and watched her, and Lucy knew she was worried. Lucy's entire family was worried about her. The nervous energy she had always had was worse the longer she was at home with nothing to do and because Leo was gone from her life.

Tomorrow would have been their first month anniversary if they had gotten married the day they had planned. But instead, it was the three-week anniversary of when she lost him and the entire world she was creating.

His face when he accused her of trying to kill Amelia still brought tears to her eyes. It still caused her breath to stop, and her body would start to shake. Biting her lip, she tried to make it stop, but the panic washed over her like it was happening all over again.

"Lucy? Are you okay?" She could hear Harper's voice, but she was back in Leo's dining room. This time she was alone with Amelia, and this time nobody could save her from Lucy.

Breathing was impossible, and sheer darkness engulfed her.

CHAPTER THIRTY-THREE

THE SCENE that met Leo's eyes as he walked into Lucy's doctor's office told him he had been right to worry. Lucy had been standing stock still in the middle of the room, and Harper had been rushing at her to knock her down.

Lucy was now showing her pregnancy under the white sweatshirt and black leggings. Her chocolate locks were in a ponytail.

Before he could get to her, Harper grabbed Lucy as her body dropped lifeless to the floor. Harper's body hit the ground first, letting her sister fall on top of her. The nurse at the desk was on the phone and watched everything that was happening.

"Lucy!" Harper yelled at her sister and slapped her cheeks. Lucy was laying on her, unmoving. "Wake up, Lucy!"

"What happened?" Leo fell to his knees beside them.

"I don't know. She was pacing and then stopped. I knew she was fainting; I just knew." Harper was rubbing Lucy's arms as she spoke, and tears of concern were running down her cheeks. It was a different side of Lucy's older sister that Leo had never seen, the concern and caring.

"Is it the babies?" he asked.

Before she could answer, emergency workers rushed into the room and lifted Lucy onto a stretcher with Leo and Harper following close behind. But when they pushed her into a room, neither were allowed to follow.

"I don't know what happened. I was right there watching her." Harper started to kick at the wall between her and her sister.

"Has this happened before?" His eyes were on the door, not the sister.

"No, but Agatha said she hasn't been eating much. I even stopped making food so that she would eat, but she doesn't. I'm worried for her and the babies." He could hear the tears in her voice, but she didn't look away from her foot, still kicking the wall.

"I'm sorry I didn't let you see her that week." No need to say which week, they both knew.

"It was better I was not there. We used to be best friends. I don't know if we will get that back again." She turned and leaned against the wall, then slid down it so she was sitting on the floor, her knees up to her chest.

"What happened?" He had to know. Lucy said she didn't know, but Harper had to.

"When I was working for Kaine, I made her do too much—so much she wasn't even getting to sleep some nights. So, I hired people because I didn't want her to work all the time. Then Kaine and I agreed to cut back on our workloads. I dropped events. But I just did it; I never asked her about it. I should have talked to her." Harper had stopped kicking but was still looking at the wall.

"Yes, you should have," he agreed, wondering if miscommunication could have been all it was.

"For years she never cared. When did she start caring? I've messed up everything for Lucy, and now I will never get her back. I'll never get to work with her again, she says she doesn't ever want to cook again."

"She will cook again."

"No, she quit because she thought I didn't want her. It's been months, and she never talked to me about it. She was my best friend once, but now she barely talks to me. Or anyone. I think she's going to run away after the babies are gone." She started kicking again.

"I think running away is extreme, Harper." He touched Harper's arm, and the kicking stopped.

Harper turned and looked at him with tears in her eyes. "Lucy *is* extreme, Leo, she always has been. Since the beginning, she's been that way to hide who she really is. Since she was very young, she acted out, got in trouble. Even before Sera showed up, she smoked and drank and hung out with boys, acting out in ways that wouldn't make people look at the real reason why she is the way she is. When it came out that she has dyslexia, she let us think she had fixed it. That she had changed. She got her job and stopped partying. But she didn't fix it, because you *can't* fix it. You can only manage it, and she was only pretending to do that. And now she's stopped pretending."

"She was an excellent personal assistant, Harper. I never even questioned whether or not she could read. It never crossed my mind," Leo said. Though looking back, he saw the little things that she hid, that she adapted to help herself. She had done it so well he hadn't noticed it.

"Maby says Lucy thinks she is a danger to the babies. But what happens when Mom and Buzz have their babies? She'll take off. That's what I would do if it were me." Harper leaned against the wall.

Across from them, a door opened, and a man backed out telling everyone in the room, "I'm going to take a leak."

He turned and clearly wasn't happy to see Harper in the hallway. With the door securely closed, he smiled what Leo assumed the man thought was a flirty smile at the blonde. "Where is Luce?"

"Exam room." Harper pointed at the closed door.

"This your husband or the baby's dad?" He nodded at Leo.

"The baby's dad," Harper confirmed, then grinned for the first time since he had seen her. She got to her feet. "Leo, Kevin says his dick is bigger than yours."

"Really? Why?" Leo looked at the man, who was staring at Harper in disbelief.

"Because Kevin has a small dick but won't admit it," Harper stated like she was talking about the weather.

Leo looked at the man and then remembered Lucy telling him

about a Kevin that Aubrey was dating. Could this be the same Kevin, this snively guy? Lucy was completely right about everything about the man.

"I said no such thing. Really, man, I do not need to see your dick." He put up his hands and took a step back. "You know something? The last time I was with Luce was the night you told her to get a different job, Harper. Nice sister you are."

"You know nothing about me or my family," Harper insisted, raising her chin.

"I know that Lucy wanted to be a caterer, and that you told her she should get an office job because you didn't need her anymore. Then you hired a chef within days because she wasn't good enough for you anymore. You said you needed another chef, not a cook."

"There's no difference between the two," Harper argued and took a step toward him. Leo could tell that the words bothered Harper. "They are one and the same at Lovely Catering."

"They may do the same thing, but everyone knows who the chef was, and who wasn't. You always treated her like she was hired help until you didn't need her anymore. You only used her as long as she was useful, but when you could afford it, she wasn't good enough for you." Kevin smirked. He knew he was picking at a scab for Harper.

"I did not," Harper insisted, but her bravado was suddenly gone.

"With cleaning, she could work around you and catering. How many times did she start working on something when you were still working in the office? How many times did she sleep for an hour or two before you would call for something? Then you told her to get a job that wouldn't allow her to help you at all, a job she'd never liked. Then you stopped talking to her when she didn't help you anymore," the man said, sensing victory.

Leo looked at Harper. Had she not liked her job as his assistant? Had she just done it because she couldn't do what she wanted to do?

"*I did not,*" she snapped, then added, "She needed better then cleaning. Better hours."

"Except all she wanted to do was catering with you. Do you even know how many times she went to The Jay and kissed ass for you to get that call? For weeks and weeks, she did little shit that the dude barely cared about. Then you just dropped it as if it didn't matter. And Lucy was the one who had made that happen."

Harper's mouth dropped open in surprise, it seemed she hadn't known. Recovering from the shock she explained to him, even if she should save it for her sister, "We didn't have time. It would have been like having a restaurant and not a catering business. If I wanted a restaurant, I would have opened one. I love the freedom of catering."

"Did you ever tell her that?"

Harper sighed. "No."

"Now don't you feel stupid?" the man asked, a smirk on his lips.

"Not when you're around," she shot back at him.

He narrowed his eyes at her. "Hey!"

"How many kids do you have, Kevin?" Harper asked, all curious.

"Eight, I think. I don't really keep track." He shrugged and grinned as if he was more of a man by having so many kids. "Why?"

"Because I am going to do two things: make you never forget what you did to my sister and every girl you cheated on, and stop you from having any more kids," Harper boldly stated as she walked up to the man.

"And how are you going to do that?" he smirked, not sensing he might be in danger.

"Like this." Harper grabbed his shoulders and slammed her knee into his nuts so hard the guy's eyes rolled back in his head. Then she did it again, and then once more before he fell to the ground, grabbing himself and moaning.

"My sister is the *best* thing that ever happened to you, and you blew it, dickhead. Now I would appreciate if you never talked to her again. And every time I hear your name, I will find you and do that again, every time!" Harper turned and stalked back toward Leo, dusting off her jeans as she came.

"I hope I'm not next," Leo said while looking at the man who had wet himself and was now surrounded by nurses who were trying to question what had happened. Harper only shrugged.

"Let's see how you handle the next few hours. If you fail, you'll know it," Harper replied ominously as she watched three people help the man to his feet. He could barely remain upright.

"Why do you think I won't fail?" he asked, wondering if Harper would do that same thing to him but was sure she would.

Harper gave him a sideways look. "Because you love her."

"Why do you say that?"

"Because everyone loves Lucy. You have since I first met you. You can't not. Look at Kevin." She grinned, watching a nurse lead him away.

"I am *nothing* like that man."

"I know, he's an ass. You just act like one a lot." She grinned as if it were a joke.

"That hurts, Harper." Leo shot back her, comparing him to that man was not called for.

"Relax, Montgomery. You had the look from the beginning. Lucy was your sole focus. Why do you think you hated me so much? Because she did." She calmly waved at a woman coming out of the room Kevin had come out of. The woman looked up and down the hallway and then headed toward the exit.

"I didn't hate you; I just didn't want you hurting her."

"Ditto, man. I'm the oldest, which means I have to protect every one of my sisters. Even when they piss me off," Harper said as a nurse came out of the room that Lucy was in and looked at them both.

Without a word, he took the door and let Harper go into the room before him. Maybe Harper would be an ally. At least he hoped she would be an ally, because being on the wrong side of a Lovely was not where he wanted to be.

CHAPTER THIRTY-FOUR

"Welcome back, honey." A handsome blonde with the greenest eyes Lucy had ever seen was staring at her so intently that if she could have gotten away from him, she would have.

"From where?" she asked, wondering why her voice sounded so groggy.

"You passed out, sweetie. We have you hooked up to an IV now, and you will be good soon. Don't worry, the babies are just fine in there. Perfectly safe."

"For now." She ran a hand over them, noticing the tubes running into her left arm as she did.

"Don't worry about it." He patted her on the hand as he checked another monitor, then turned back to Lucy. A tear ran down her face. She was endangering her babies even before they entered the world.

"No tears, everything is fine. Nothing happened that can't be fixed. Nothing ever happens that can't be fixed."

"What if I feed them the wrong thing?" Lucy asked, her biggest fear.

"I don't think you ever will." He sounded so confident, but he didn't know Lucy.

"How do you know? You don't know me."

"Because you're asking, and you still have months left in this pregnancy. You'll do just fine," he assured her.

"I … I can't read," she admitted. She had never said it out loud before.

"Nor could my grandma, and she raised ten kids, five of which were still in school when my grandpa died. If she can do it, so can you," the man said, no judgement about her confession.

"What if they have allergies?"

"If they do, just ask every question you can think of to the doctor who diagnoses them. Talk to friends and family. Someone who has allergies and can help you out. The great thing about parenting is that so many others are in the same boat as you. You're really never alone," the nurse said and looked at her chart.

"I have no money and don't have a job anymore. I'm broke." The words just spilled out of her; she wasn't able to stop them.

"Money doesn't raise kids; love does. You have all the love in the world, and these babies will have the best life ever."

Watching him, she said, "You seem to have all the answers."

"I just have some of them. I don't know everything. New moms are full of worry and doubt—you're not the first or the last. Just remember to follow your heart, not your mind. Your mind tends to overthink things, but your heart doesn't. It just knows," he assured her, probably realizing that she needed to talk more than anything else right then.

She was skeptical. "My heart has led me astray before."

"Or has it just been a part of your path? Sometimes it isn't straight, you know. Corners make life interesting." He smiled.

"That's a different way to look at it."

"Sometimes being different is what makes you you." He closed out of the computer, spun in his chair, and looked at Lucy. "Are you ready for company? There are some people in the hall waiting to make sure you're okay."

"I don't think I will get any more ready." She smiled at him. "What's your name?"

"Owen." He smiled and waved and headed for the door.

Once the door was open, her mind went blank as Harper rushed in, followed closely by Leo. Leo was in a suit and tie, and his eyes were on her with a look of concern. How he could look even better, she didn't know, but she figured he would be disappointed with how she looked. Again, in a hospital bed.

"Are you okay?" Harper asked as she rushed to her bed.

"Yes, I think so. Babies are great." She couldn't take her eyes off Leo.

"I am sorry, Lucy, so sorry. I am an idiot who took you for granted and then didn't talk to you about our business, even after I realized juat how much of our business you were. I may have been the chef, but you were the heart," Harper stated as if they were in the middle of a conversation Lucy couldn't remember starting.

"What?" She looked at her sister. Her words made no sense at all.

"Lovely Catering is *ours*, and I want you back. I want what we had except I want us to be partners. I swear I will talk to you about everything, more than everything," Harper promised.

"I can't, Harper," Lucy argued.

"Leo admits that it was a mistake, one that will never happen again. How do I know? Because from here on out, there will be no almonds, nuts, or even milk in anything from Lovely Catering or in any house where a Lovely lives," Harper stated with her hand over her heart, then pulled out her phone. "I am sending a text to everyone."

"Harper ..." she started, but Harper put up her hand to stop her.

"Kevin and I talked. He said some things that were true about how I treated you. I'm going to change," Harper confessed and hugged Lucy to her.

"Kevin? When?" Lucy was not following the conversation at all.

Harper sighed. "A few minutes ago. He won't be an issue anymore. I think it will finally stick that he has to leave you alone."

"Is he alive?" Lucy hesitantly asked. Harper could go overboard.

"Of course, but with any luck, Pam might be having his last kid." She smiled, then tried to hide it with her hand.

"Poor Pam." Lucy felt sorry for the woman who was stuck with

Kevin forever through a child. There was no way she would ever tell her own kids about him.

"Oh, come on. Remember her stealing that weird guy from Buzz like three years ago? And she's been trying to steal Kevin since high school. See what happens when dreams come true?" Harper said, touching Lucy's cheek.

"I forgot about her taking Brandon from Buzz." Lucy smiled. "Buzz has no luck in love."

"Until Jonas. Pretty lucky there." Harper kissed her forehead and whispered, "Like you."

"Harps …" Lucy wasn't up for telling another sister that Leo didn't love her, especially with him in the room.

"I'm going to call everyone and tell them you're okay. I'll leave Sera for last since she'll be here in a heartbeat after I tell her. Be ready." Harped playfully ran her shoulder into Leo's on the way past.

His eyes were on the blonde as she did it, then went back to Lucy as Harper shut the door behind her, leaving them alone.

"Leo."

Leo silently walked to the bed and sat down on the edge, took her hand in his, and squeezed it. "I'm just going to try what Harper did." He took a breath. "I'm sorry, Lucy. I overreacted and treated you like my personal assistant instead of my future wife. I should have talked to you, involved you when I was taking Amelia to the doctor. I let you believe that you were a danger to my family because of one mistake."

"I understand, Leo. I *am* dangerous. I see that now," Lucy admitted.

"You're anything but dangerous, Lucy. You made a mistake. But now that we all know about your reading, we can help you," he said.

She turned away from him, hating that he knew. Had Harper told him while they'd waited? Had it been someone else? But now he knew how stupid she was. "It shouldn't take everyone helping me to not be a danger to your kids."

Leo took her chin in his hand and gently turned her to face him. Their eyes met and held for a moment.

"Lucy, when Aubrey and Alexis were five and two, they nearly died.

Kelly and I were separated, and I had the girls for the weekend. I was upset with Kelly for something, I can't even remember anymore, but it made me miss a red light. We were hit by not one, but two cars. Both girls were in the hospital for a few days. For months I blamed myself. I was at fault," he said.

Lucy took his hand from her chin and held it tight. "Car accidents happen all the time. The girls were okay in the end, that is what is important. They probably don't even remember it."

"Just like what happened with Amelia, Lucy. We will learn from it and get over it," he promised.

"I won't," she whispered. She still thought about it every day.

He sat down on the edge of her bed, still holding her hand. "And maybe that's okay because it will always be in the back of your mind, making it twice as hard for it to happen again."

"What if it does?"

"We will be okay then also. Once you know how to deal with a reaction, we'll all know how to. Do you want to learn?" he asked.

"Yes, very much so." She nodded, even if she couldn't be a part of Amelia's life anymore.

He smiled at her. "I will teach you under one condition."

She looked at him nervously. "What?"

"That you marry me." He pulled her ring from his pants pocket and adjusted her hands until he could slip it on her finger.

Staring at it in disbelief, she answered truthfully, "Leo, I can't. I can't marry you for your kids anymore. I just can't."

"I am not asking you for my kids, Lucy. In fact, I haven't needed to marry you for my kids since not long after you got out of the hospital from your fall. Stacy isn't moving any more, she was probably never going to in the first place. It was just another way to get more money. Since then, I have wanted to marry you for you. I love you, Lucy, everything about you. And you are completely different than the woman who agreed to marry me a month ago. I don't want her, I want you."

"But ..." She started to protest. She was the same person, after all.

"To tell you the truth, I only hired you so I could sleep with you." He bit his lip at the admission.

"What?" He never once made any advances toward her, not once.

"I wanted you, and I didn't care how bad that looked. But within days I found out you were married and not interested in me at all. So instead, I settled for a great personal assistant." He pushed her hair away from her face, his fingers brushing her cheek.

"But I'm not," she admitted. She wasn't very good at her job.

"I haven't been able to find anyone else that comes close to the great job you did. I've had Aubrey working for me when she's not in school. She hates it," he told her, surprising her that he hadn't hired someone right away when she'd quit.

"I'm not surprised. Why didn't you think I was interested in you?"

"Because you never once let on that you were. You were nothing but professional around me," he said simply.

"I really thought you were good-looking," she admitted, though she hadn't really even let herself look until he asked about a wife. She hadn't been interested in a businessman.

"But?" He smiled, waiting.

"But you were not my type," she said, it was the truth, after all. "Though you are. You're the rebel without a cause that I like. You just don't let him out much."

"We were both hiding who we really were and almost missed each other. When I asked you to find someone for me to marry, I asked you because I wanted someone just like you. But you were married, so I figured you would know a lot of women like you."

She looked at him shyly. "I don't. I only ever had me on the list. I was never able to come up with another name."

"I told you that I only needed one, and yours is the perfect one. The one I wanted." He leaned down and kissed her on the lips.

"You don't want to marry me," she said again, just needing him to say that he wanted her, that he loved her.

"Lucy, I want to marry you even more now than I did in that conference room, which is hard to believe because it was the only thing I wanted that day. That and to get you naked." He smiled.

"But you said you were willing to not have sex with me," she reminded him.

"I was going to break that promise. But neither of us would've regretted it." He kissed her again.

She felt herself blush at his words. He was right, she wasn't going to regret sleeping with him.

CHAPTER THIRTY-FIVE

LEO LOVED that she blushed at his words. Hell, he loved everything about her. He had missed her more than he was willing to admit.

"Lucy Maud, are you okay?" Sera suddenly pushed into the room.

"I am fine, Sera, and so are the babies." Lucy's words were said as fast as she could, as if she were a teenager in trouble.

"That's what Harper said, but I don't actually believe it." Her eyes were only for her daughter as she rushed the bed.

"Sera, I am fine. Leo is here," Lucy said.

He was sure he'd just been thrown under the bus as a distraction for her mother. After the last time they had spoken, he was sure Sera Dean did not want to see him in her daughter's room. She probably never wanted to see him again.

"Do not try and distract me with him. What happened?" Sera wedged herself between them, causing Leo to get off the bed to let Sera do what she needed.

"I fainted. Something about low blood sugar, and I don't remember." Lucy waved her hand in the air as if that explained anything.

"As if you have forgotten. What did he say?" Sera demanded.

"She. My doctor just happens to be a woman," Lucy said, not answering the question.

"What did *she* say?" Sera tried again, a little bit angrier than before.

"I have to eat more. There you have it, just like you said over and over again. What do you want me to say, 'you are right'?" Lucy crossed her arms and glared at her mother.

"Yes, that is exactly what I want you to say. Then, I want you to eat more. Have they fed you yet?" Sera looked around the room for evidence that she had eaten.

"No."

"Why not?! What are they waiting for?" Sera made a circle around the room and headed for the door. "I will go find you something to eat."

"Sera, no," Lucy argued halfheartedly.

"Really, Lucy? You already forgot? I'm always right." She pushed out of the room with a smug look on her face.

Lucy scolded him the instant the woman was out of the room. "You were supposed to deflect."

"I didn't know I was supposed to deflect," he argued, because he had no clue.

"I pointed out you were here; that was your cue!" she stated as if she had told him before, and he just wasn't getting it.

Sitting back down on the bed, he took her hand and kissed her fingers. "Maybe we need to talk about this."

Lucy's twin came into the room through the open door. "Talk about what?"

Leo looked at the woman who was wearing nearly the exact outfit Lucy was, though hers was dressier, like she had been at the college when she got the call. He was beginning to think that the sisters didn't even notice that they did it.

"When to deflect," he informed the new arrival, who was followed closely by her husband.

"Whenever Sera has that look in her eye, deflect," Mabel stated.

"Whenever she is staring at the woman you love intently, deflect." Cliff hugged his wife to him and kissed her head.

"Nearly any intense look from Sera needs deflection," Mabel argued back.

"Not always. Sometimes she's just trying to get you to crack," Cliff stated which made his wife nod in agreement.

"She's always trying to get you to crack!" Lucy threw up her arms.

"You back with Luce, then?" Cliff asked him.

"I am, we are. Back to getting married." He held up Lucy's hand with his ring on it. Back where it belonged.

"Wait, what? When?" Sera hurried back into the room, carrying an armful of vending machine candy and chips.

"Soon, once we can start planning it again. I don't know if we want to wait until the babies come or not." He looked over at Lucy, who just shrugged in response.

"There will be no waiting. I'll get started on planning everything. You two don't worry about anything."

"Sera, it can wait. I want to plan it," Lucy argued.

"Harper will be on food, and we will have it at the cathedral."

"No cathedral!" Lucy and Mabel said together and glared at their mom.

"But ..."

"No cathedral. Just a little gathering of friends and family, and by that, I mean *just* family."

"Lucy, how about we plan it for our backyard in a few weeks?" Leo said, hoping that by then, Lucy would be off bed rest, and the weather would be nice enough to have it outside.

"Backyard? It could work. I mean, it's no cathedral, though," Sera said and dropped her armload of snacks on Lucy's lap, then gave Leo a hug.

"The outdoors is god's cathedral," Cliff informed Sera.

"Honey, I think cathedrals are actually god's cathedral," Mabel argued with him.

"What was there before cathedrals then?" Cliff asked her.

"They had something, I'm sure," Mabel said, not letting her husband have the win.

"Fine, the backyard next weekend. I can do that," Sera said, and he wondered if she had realized she pushed up the wedding date by weeks. Not that he was complaining; he should have married Lucy a month ago.

"Do what?" Harper walked back into the room, this time with Agatha. Suddenly, the room was getting crowded, but nobody seemed to notice.

Instantly, Harper walked over to her sister and gave her a hug, causing everyone in the room to stop talking and watch. Once she let go and walked away with a candy bar in her hand, she gave them all a questioning look.

Sera took the attention away from her by answering the question. "Saturday, Lucy and Leo are getting married."

"You said next weekend," Mabel said in confusion.

"Saturday *is* next weekend." Sera shrugged and started to plan. Already she was digging out her wedding planner that she was still carrying around months after her own wedding. Instantly she opened it and started paging through it, smiling.

Turning to Lucy, Leo opened a bag of chips for her and asked, "Are you okay with this?"

"I have to be. Sera's got it planned already." She smiled and sat up a little to grab the chips.

"But do you want this?" He needed to know. She hadn't actually said she wanted to marry him, and now he felt like everyone was pressuring her into it.

"Of course, I want this, Leo. I love you and want to be your wife, your *real* one."

"There will never again be anything fake between us," he promised before kissing her gently. Then he started to feed her chips. She would need her strength for her mother's wedding planning.

CHAPTER THIRTY-SIX

LUCY STOOD in Leo's office, watching the rain hit the window in sheets. She wished she could hear it hitting the window—she loved that sound. Today was her first day off bed rest, and she was happy to be able to do what she wanted. She just wished she hadn't said she would come into work.

Leo was gone to a meeting and would be back soon, but she wasn't afraid to be caught in his office anymore. In fact, today she was looking forward to it.

It had been five days since the wedding, both of them. In true Lovely fashion, she and Leo and been married before the actual marriage. She had been sure Cliff had forgotten to plan the surprise early wedding.

She and Leo had stayed at the Lovely house because they were getting up early to start the food. Harper had insisted on catering and wanted to do it with her sisters again, all of them. All the sisters had chosen to stay, and so had all husbands. The Lovely house was once again full, with men everywhere. Even Sera had stayed, and she had chosen to sleep on the couch. Harrison hadn't been happy about it and hadn't stayed, instead taking Emma and Violet home for the night.

When she had opened her eyes at 4:00 a.m., she had been disappointed that Cliff hadn't woken them in the night to start their lives together like every other sister. Climbing from bed, she had left Leo sleeping and headed downstairs. At that time, she had accidentally woken Sera when she had made too much noise in the kitchen. It was then that she had grumbled about being tired-looking and went home.

Soon after, Harper got up and then slowly, each sister showed up until the kitchen felt like old times, and she completely forgot that it was her wedding they were prepping for.

At 6:00 a.m., Cliff had walked in the kitchen dragging the judge, the same judge that had married everyone. And he still wasn't happy to be there, even if it was a better hour than most of the others' weddings.

Leo had been woken up, and within minutes they had been married in front of every sister and spouse. Even Aubrey and Alexis had been there.

After kissing her groom, she had gone back to work. If only for about a minute before Leo carried her to the living room since she wasn't supposed to be prepping for her own wedding. She was still on bed rest.

The rest of the day went by in a blur, even the wedding at the cathedral hadn't been as bad as the others that had been there. Because despite every no, Sera heard yes. A small wedding in the backyard had quickly morphed into a big event at the same cathedral Sera and Mabel had been married at months before. Lucy was a little nervous for Agatha, Emma, and Violet because Sera was uncontrollable now. Looking back on all the weddings, she decided Sera had been uncontrollable the entire time.

Leo rushed into the office as he always did, not even noticing her, but she noticed him, all gorgeous and in control as always. How she hadn't found him mouthwateringly beautiful since day one, she didn't know.

Mostly she blamed it on him not acting like who he really was around her. Who knew the womanizing, name-forgetting, player was actually the devoted, overprotective, and tattooed man he was? She did now.

"Lucy, we have to talk. I was just in a meeting with HR, and we have a problem." Leo turned his chair until he was facing her. He had noticed her there after all.

"What did they say?" She walked around to her chair. She liked how his eyes tracked her movements.

"There was a complaint filed about me," he said with a frown as she walked to the door that was between their offices, a door that was always open. Only when he was in important meetings was it closed until today.

"By who?" She turned back to him.

"Someone named Macy. I have never heard of a Macy, and neither have they." He picked up his pen and tapped it on the desk.

"Macy, Macy, Macy," she said over and over as if she was trying to come up with a person to go with the name as she walked toward him.

He shook his head. "We don't have a Macy here."

"What's the complaint about?" She bypassed her usual chair and went around his desk.

"That I had sex with her in my office." He mindlessly backed his chair up so she could get a better look at the note he brought in.

"Did you?" She leaned over and looked at the paper, wondering if Leo realized she wasn't reading it.

"Of course not. I have never had sex in my office," he stated and tossed the pen down.

"Because you don't want to?" she asked, turning to him.

"Because I'm not having sex with anyone but you."

She quirked an eyebrow at him. "You want to have sex with me?"

"Seriously? You have to ask, Lucy? I have so many plans for when you're off bed rest."

That got her attention. "Really? Like what?"

"Like stripping you naked and keeping you in bed for a week. Making love to you in every room I can in our house. Licking your entire body until you can't breathe except to beg me to take you again and again."

"So specific, yet nothing about here ... Macy will be disappointed."

She pushed aside all his papers as she hopped onto the desk, causing her skirt to ride up her bare legs.

Leo ran his hands up her legs as he looked at them. "Let her be."

Pouting, she pulled him close on his rolling office chair. Leaning down, she licked his ear before whispering, "Do you remember calling me Macy for the first two weeks I worked for you?"

"No."

"You did, every single day." She unbuttoned her shirt slowly, then pulled it from the waist of her skirt.

"What are you doing, Lucy?" he asked in a shaky voice, but his hands kept moving up until they cupped her bare breasts.

"Making Macy's prediction come true." She pulled his tie free and tossed it on the floor.

"Bed rest, Lucy," he hissed, but suddenly, his hands were pushing hers away as he ripped open his own shirt and stood up.

Licking her lips, she said huskily, "It's over."

Leo put his hands on either side of her, then braced himself as he looked into her eyes. Just as she was starting to think she'd made a mistake, his lips crashed into hers. Wrapping her arms around him, she kissed him back with the same fervor as she always did.

She loved how much he couldn't control himself with her but then always managed to stop before they went too far. Because after five days of marriage and three days of engagement, they had yet to have sex. Bed rest was Lucy's enemy until today. Today, she was free.

Never in a million years would she have thought she was going to marry a man she had never had sex with. Their entire relationship had gone completely different than any of her others, which might've been why it was going to work out. For once, the entire relationship wasn't about sex; it was about everything else, and sex was an added bonus.

A bonus she wanted right now. She didn't want to wait until they got home, until the kids were in bed, or until she was exhausted and only wanted to sleep. She wanted it now.

Leo's hands were on her breasts, quickly followed by his mouth. His tongue made her moan and squirm. As he licked and sucked his way to her other breast, he slid her skirt even farther up her legs, his fingers brushing her wet folds. His groan told her he appreciated that she wasn't wearing panties.

"You are gorgeous, Lucy," he whispered as his fingers brushed her clit, causing her hips to buck.

He pushed her flat on her back and sat down heavy in his chair. Before she could question what he was doing, he wrapped his arms around her legs and pulled her to the edge of the desk. His mouth replaced his fingers, bringing a low growl from her as his talented tongue did things to her that made her jerk and writhe on the desk.

When his finger slipped into her heat, she tried to stop it, but within moments, waves of pleasure were coursing through her body. Screaming his name as she came, she completely forgot that they were in his office. Or didn't care.

"Leo, Leo, I need …" She didn't even get the words out before his cock slid into her. Exactly what she wanted.

Before she could wrap her legs around him, he pressed them against his chest. He gripped her hips while sliding in and out in a slow, steady thrust, each one causing a ripple of pleasure to course through her when he was fulling sheathed inside of her.

Trying and failing to grip his desk to give herself leverage, she looked into his face. Instantly, she knew he was holding back, that he wanted to be gentle with her. Whether it was because it was the first time or because she was pregnant, she didn't know, nor did she care. She didn't want him to hold back.

"Hard, Leo, hard," she said and watched him let go.

Suddenly, she couldn't tell anymore where she ended, and he began or who was moaning and who was screaming. All she knew was that she was coming, and it wasn't stopping. Her hips jerked and twisted, and Leo swore loudly as his entire body stiffened and held her still as his cock pulsed deep inside her body, causing her to jerk again.

When both of their bodies calmed down, Leo sat her up slowly. Then he kissed her as he sat down in his chair, pulling her with him. Nestling on his lap, she nuzzled into his shoulder, kissing it lightly as she did.

Leo ran his fingers up and down her bare spine. "You are Macy, aren't you?"

"I am." She kissed his shoulder and the tattoo that started there.

Pulling her tighter to him, he asked in confusion. "You planned this?"

"Yes."

"Why? We have a house and a bed. Or a hotel and a bed." It seemed he needed a bed.

She nipped his shoulder and laughed as she leaned back and looked him in the eyes. "And you never once thought about having sex on this desk? Not even once?"

"Maybe once." He grinned and pushed the hair off her face, hair she was sure looked like sex hair.

"With Macy?" Getting off his lap, she grabbed her shirt from the floor and slipped it on as he pulled up his boxers and pants.

"With Lucy and *only* Lucy. Because Macy feels like a combination of your and Mabel's names. I only think of Mabel as my sister-in-law. Lucy has my heart." He kissed her nose as he said it and started buttoning up her shirt.

"I love you, Leo." She wrapped her arms around him again, and he pulled her back onto his lap.

"I love you, Lucy Montgomery." He ran his thumb over her lips. "But I am firing you."

In shock, she pulled away from him. "Because we had sex on the desk?"

"Because you don't like working here. When you agreed to marry me, I told you it was up to you if you work or not. I didn't mention, but should have, that you can work wherever you want to. I want you happy, and catering makes you happy," Leo insisted.

"Are you sure?" she asked, her chin quivering because she wanted to go back to working with Harper. She still hated working as a personal assistant. No matter how much she loved Leo and wanted to spend every moment with him. Her heart just wasn't in office work. It was still in the kitchen.

"You want to go back, Lucy, and you only told her no because of me. But I will still be madly and deeply in love with you when you're a caterer." He kissed her softly. "I seem to have asked my assistant for a wife, and the only woman she found was this caterer."

"How did she do?" she dared to ask.

"Perfectly," was all he said before pulling her back into his arms.

It was exactly how she felt about it. Nothing had ever been so perfect.

EPILOGUE

Lucy looked around the kitchen, loving that they were prepping at the Lovely house again. It was just like old times: over half the sisters helping, and the rest were around, only not actually helping. Emma and Mabel were in the middle of a movie that they couldn't stop watching, or so they said.

"Do you have those done?" Harper shot at her.

She had been working on making an appetizer for an hour. The dish was easy to make but allowed her to sit as she made it. So she had chosen to make them.

"Yes, just need to get them in the fridge," Lucy informed her with a smile.

"There's no room. Put them in the cooler in the van." Harper waved her off, though the "van" was her Land Rover. They were not going to tell Kaine about it, but Lucy was sure he knew.

"Can someone else?" she asked, rubbing her back that was killing her.

The twins hadn't given her much trouble over the last few months, until now. And maybe last week, when she had Leo take her to the hospital in error. So, she wasn't complaining today in hopes of not repeating that again.

"Just do it, Lucy," Harper stated, her concentration on moving the stuffed pork chops from the pan to the warmer.

"I'm pregnant, Harps," she reminded the woman.

"And who's fault was that? Not mine. I wasn't there." Harper didn't even turn away from her task as she spoke.

"Really, Harper? You are the only one in this room who's not pregnant," Buzz stated from her spot at the table. She wasn't actually helping either, just entertaining. Or so she said.

"Fine, but if I ever get knocked up, you will all be helping for the entire eight months I am carrying that kid." Harper pointed at Sera, Buzz, and Lucy.

"It's nine months," Sera said from her place cutting up celery sticks.

"Not when I have a kid. Seven or eight months tops. I don't have time for nine months. I'm the only one who works around here, you know." She stomped over to Lucy and grabbed the container from her.

Once she was close enough to grab the container, Lucy had a feeling she would never forget for the rest of her life. It was the feeling of warm water running down her legs, a lot of water. Looking down, she saw there was a nice-sized puddle, and Harper's canvas-clad foot was in the middle of it.

"Did you just pee on me?" Harper's brown eyes glared at her. "Tell me you peed on me!"

Lucy tried not to laugh at Harper's expression. "No, I didn't."

"Lucy, your water broke!" Sera yelled and jumped up from the counter.

"Baby marinade? You got *baby marinade* all over me?!" Harper yelled at the celling.

Emma, Mabel, and even Agatha rushed into the room faster than Lucy thought possible. Sera directed Emma to take the container to the Land Rover and rushed over to take Lucy's arm.

"Are you in pain?" she asked as she sat her down at the table.

"No, and I thought I would be." Lucy rubbed her stomach as her lower half started to feel cold.

"It's coming," Agatha stated as if she knew, earning her glares from Sera and Lucy.

Harper was in the same spot she had been in a moment before, trying to get her shoe off without touching it. It was taking more effort than it should have and was spreading the wetness into a bigger puddle.

"Agatha, shush. So, we have to get you to the hospital," Sera said.

"No way! She's helping me today. I need her! She can have the babies tomorrow. We have nothing planned tomorrow," Harper whined as she finally got her shoes off and left them laying in the puddle. She started peeling off a sock with her fingertips.

"It doesn't work that way," Sera informed her, rolling her eyes.

"She knows where she's needed, Sera, here. Lucy, change pants and start with the potatoes." Harper tossed the second sock in the puddle and waved at the area by the stove.

"She's off the clock," Maby announced and started helping Lucy to her feet.

"No, come on, I need her!" Harper whined again as she pulled off her pants and tossed them into the pile also. Now in her underwear, she stared at her little sister, her business partner. "You planned this, didn't you?"

"I didn't. I want to be here, but the babies ..." Lucy tried to explain.

"How could she have planned this?" Buzz asked.

"Easy, Buzz. She found a way to trigger it to start," Harper accused, trying not to smile.

"Like what?" Lucy asked, raising an eyebrow at her.

"Sex. Everyone knows that's the trigger. Good sex," Harper replied, folding her arms over her chest.

"Does it have to be good?" Mabel asked curiously.

"Yes, Lucy. Why, did you have sex recently?" Harper demanded.

"Not saying." She knew she had turned red, completely red.

"Lucy, you know better than to have sex when you're pregnant!" Harper wailed.

"I, um, hadn't heard that," Lucy said because she hadn't. Not that it had pushed her into labor over the last two months anyway. Just today.

"When?! When did you have sex?" Harper demanded.

Lucy knew she was still blushing, realizing it had only been four hours ago. And if good sex triggered labor, then labor was going to happen after their office "meeting."

Clearing her throat, she countered, "That is a myth. We have had plenty of good sex in the last two months, and nothing happened … until today."

"Shoot, this was really working in my favor." Buzz sat down heavily on the stool Sera had abandoned and took a celery stick.

"Sorry, Buzzy," Lucy said. At five months along, Buzz had been miserable for over half her pregnancy already, and the remaining months weren't looking to get any better for her. Now her plan to trigger labor was out the window.

Buzz took a loud bite and then grinned. "So, a *lot* of good sex, Lucy?"

"Shut up, Buzz," Lucy hissed, not wanting to talk about it.

Mabel took out her phone. "We had better call Leo."

"Shoot, he's going to be pissed. This was not on his schedule today," Lucy said, because despite not working for him, she still kept a mental copy of his schedule out of habit.

"Well, pencil it in, Lucy! It's happening." Sera gave her a hug as they started for the door, leaving Harper alone, mad, and taking off her shirt to throw in the pile with the rest of her clothes. Lucy was sure she would never hear the end of this one.

EIGHT HOURS later it had happened, and their family of six became a family of eight. Both exes had brought their respective children to see them. Kelly had held both of the babies and gushed over how cute they were, while Stacy hadn't even come into the room with the girls.

Since they had gotten married, Leo and Lucy had decided to try and get more time with the girls, which had been met with resistance from Stacy. But they were getting the kids twice as much as Leo had before they'd gotten married.

It had taken another few hours to get every Lovely to leave, many coming back the instant they thought everyone was gone. Finally, Harrison took Sera home, promising to keep her there until at least the morning.

"Can I bring up how you were not supposed to work hard today?" Leo stated, his arms crossed. The call from Mabel had him panicking and leaving in the middle of a delicate negotiation, one that had worked itself out after he had rushed to the hospital, only to beat Lucy there—by half an hour.

"I didn't work hard. Nothing I hadn't done before," Lucy stated.

"That's not the definition of 'hard' when you are eight months pregnant with twins," he said, as always. She wasn't one for not working hard.

"Okay, so I wasn't actually thinking they would come today. The doctors said nothing about today," she argued. It wasn't a good argument, but it was the one she was going with.

"They said 'anytime.'"

"That doesn't mean *today*," she said and tapped on the railing of the bed.

He gave her a look of disbelief. "Are you just going to talk around this?"

"Yes." She smiled at him. "Can I hold a baby?"

He had lost the argument, but he still had two healthy baby boys. "Of course, which one?"

"Baby A, unless we're going with A names, in which case they'd both be baby A," she answered.

"No A's." Leo picked up a sleeping baby and handed him to Lucy, who was holding out her arms and wiggling her fingers in anticipation.

"I want different letters. Other than that, you can choose," she said for the first time. Before, she'd always wanted matchy-matchy names.

"You mean like Lucy and Mabel?" Handing her the first baby, he was surprised at how big they were with how small she'd been when she was carrying them.

"We cannot name them that. I can't say I don't love the combination, but something else," she joked as she unwrapped the tightly bundled baby so that she could look at his arms and legs and fingers and toes.

"You're vetoing us naming our twins after your favorite sister?" He picked up the other baby and picked out every feature that was his wife in the tiny face. Nearly everything.

"I guess if you want Harper, Harper one will be." She didn't even look up, she was so engrossed in her baby.

"Is she back to being your best friend then?" he asked, sitting down on the bed and looking at her.

"Yes, she is. We talked about what our expectations for the company are and who will do what and when. It was easy once we started." They were now in constant communication about the business. Harper was no longer the boss and in charge; it was a true partnership.

"Good. Dealing with you two fighting was hard."

"It was."

"But I'm vetoing Harper. One Harper is more than enough. I want Luke," he said, remembering her naming them Luke and Maynard months before. The combination was too much, but Luke was adorably close to Lucy.

"Luke," she said the name slowly while looking at the baby in his arms. Lucy then looked at the baby on her lap and kissed his forehead before saying, "This one is Owen."

"I thought you didn't care?" he teased.

She shrugged. "He looks like an Owen."

He knew she only said that because they were identical. They both actually looked a lot like her and Mabel. He hoped that they would grow up as close as she and her sister were, because he loved how close she was with her sister, and everyone else in the family.

"Luke and Owen. That was easy." She smiled and looked at the baby he was holding.

"Everything is easy with you, Lucy Lovely." He kissed her smiling lips.

"Montgomery," she corrected.

"You will always be Lovely to me." He kissed her again, just as both the boys started to cry at once.

Life was going to be interesting now, but at least he had her by his side for it.

The End

Only one sister remains single, see her love story in <u>Falling into a Second Chance</u>. Agatha meets her match when an old flame moves in across the street.

ABOUT ALIE GARNETT

I love to read and prefer a little spice in those books. I am lucky enough to live on a small hobby farm in northern Minnesota with her husband and two kids. I enjoy spending time in the pasture with my two mini horses and one fainting goat (who doesn't actually faint). When I'm not writing, I'm busy trying to do all the things I didn't get to while writing. Or maybe I wouldn't have gotten to them anyway, because its laundry, dishes and fun things like that.

ALSO BY ALIE GARNETT

<u>Indulge</u>

Craving Winter

Enticing Aurora

<u>Landstad, ND</u>

Invisible

Irresistible

Impulsive

Insuppressible

Intriguing

Imperfect

Irreplaceable

<u>The Great Lovely Falls</u>

Falling for the Single Mom

Falling for his Best Friends Sister

Falling for the Boss

Falling for his Step-Sister

Falling for his Fake Wife

Falling into a Second Chance

<u>Hart Series</u>

Seeing her Pain

Her Favor

Max Valentine is Looking at Me!

Keeping her Safe

<u>Stand Alone</u>

Romancing the Doctor